HIGH PRAISE FOR KATIE MAXWELL!

THEY WEAR WHAT UNDER THEIR KILTS?

"Welcome back to the sidesplitting universe of Emily Williams. . . . [This is] a larky addition that won't disappoint teens hooked by the first book."

—*Booklist*

"A complete blast to read."

—*RT BOOKclub*

"A must-have book, as Emily's antics cannot be missed."
—Erica Soroco, teen correspondent for
The Press Enterprise

"Maxwell delivers a character that speaks her mind while making you laugh out loud. . . . Maxwell's novel is a real trip."

—*The Barnes & Noble Review*

MORE PRAISE FOR KATIE MAXWELL!

THE YEAR MY LIFE WENT DOWN THE LOO

"*The Year My Life Went Down the Loo* is a treat! Laugh-out-loud funny, full of sly wit and humor, poignant, realistic teenage angst, and expertly drawn characters, the book is impossible to put down."

—*Romance Reviews Today*

"Gripping, smart-alecky, shocking . . . and at the same time tender. A brilliant debut by Katie Maxwell in the Young Adult forum!"

—*KLIATT*

"Girls of all ages will find themselves laughing out loud at Emily's crazy antics and experiences, but will also find themselves relating to [her]. A great start to a great new series."

—Erica Sorocco, teen correspondent
for *The Press Enterprise*

"Refreshing . . . true to life, dealing with an average teenage girl's issues instead of the mild and bland subjects covered in many other YA novels. Girls will laugh, sigh and squeal aloud as they embark upon Emily's journey."

—*BOOKclub*

REASONS MY E-MAILS ABOUT FANG ARE BETTER THAN OTHER BF E-MAILS

1. First, Fang isn't really my BF. You know how girls who have BFs go on and on and on about them, telling you everything about how fabu they are, and what shirts they are wearing on that day, and how cute their bods are, yadda yadda yadda, until you want to set your hair on fire rather than listen to any more? Well, you won't find that here. Except maybe a reference to Fang's behind. Because it really is adorable. So that doesn't count.

2. I don't just talk about what a hottie he is—I also give you Deep Emotional Insight into his Deep Emotional Nature, which is just . . . well, Deep. In an Emotional kind of way. Trust me on this, 'K?

3. Unfortunately, where there's Fang, there's bound to be Audrey, his GF from New Zealand. So you get to hear about her, too, especially my plans to (bwahahahahah!) find her another boyfriend.

4. Fang does interesting things, like visits me at work (he liked the bird skeletons—ew!), takes Audrey and me to cool tourist spots (although he wouldn't let me push her in the river), and knows how to use a sword. How can you help but fall madly in love with him?

The Taming of the Dru

Katie Maxwell

SMOOCH NEW YORK

*My thanks to Lori and Trevor Grube for all their support,
warm fuzzies, and witty repartee over dinner,
with an extra dollop of gratitude to Trevor alone,
for telling all his girl minions about Emily.*

SMOOCH ®

September 2004

Published by

Dorchester Publishing Co., Inc.
200 Madison Avenue
New York, NY 10016

ISBN: 0-8439-5298-9

The name "SMOOCH" and its logo are trademarks of Dorchester
Publishing Co., Inc.

Printed in the United States of America.

Visit us on the web at www.smoochya.com.

The.
Taming
of the
Dru

Subject: Sooooooo coolio!
From: Emmers@britsahoy.co.uk
To: Dru@seattlegrrl.com
Date: 1 August 2004 10:23pm

Hey, chicky, I'm back from the trip to London. Ahmed at the Tongue and Groove club says hi. (Yeah, Holly's brother Peter got us into the club, which is majorly coolio, let me tell you!) Anyhoo, when I got home last night, Brother was all *I've got a secret*. You know how I hate it when he does that. Why can't I have a normal father? One that doesn't play with medieval torture devices?

"Your secret is that you get turned on by thumbscrews?" I asked, watching with more than a little concern as Brother toyed with a reproduction thumb-screw. (One of his fellow professors at Oxford has come up with a line of torture toys based on the originals. Brother says it'll make millions. I say why didn't he think of that so *we* could have millions?)

"No, of course not," he said, his Unibrow all scrunched up into a frown.

"Because if you and Mom are getting into kinky stuff, I don't want to know about it," I warned. "I'm only just managing to forget that horrible thing that Mom said to me last year."

His Unibrow furrowed even more. "What horrible thing?"

"That you guys have a healthy sex life. Bleh."

Brother sighed and looked upward for a couple of seconds, like he was praying or something. "Emily, why does every conversation I have with you end up being about sex?"

"Because you're obsessed with it," I said gently, and even patted him on the arm so he wouldn't think I hated him for it. "But that's OK; I've learned to live with it."

His hand ruffled through his hair, which probably would have formed his usual hair horn, but did I tell you he got his hair cut last week? He couldn't get in to his regular guy, so he went to a new one, Mr. Manny, who buzzed his hair instead of doing the old-guy 'do, so now Brother looks kind of like Boris Karloff. With bulgy pug eyes. "That's it, I give up. I formally renounce my fatherhood. I officially recognize the fact that even though you sprang from the fruit of my loins, I have no control over you whatsoever."

"Welcome to the real world," I said, patting him on his arm again. "So what is this news you have?"

"There's much to be said for vasectomies," he muttered as he plopped down in the chair behind his desk.

"You're quickly slipping into the *ew* zone. The news? For me? That you heard and you're not telling me?"

He sighed heavily like it was such a big deal to tell me, but finally said, "Do you remember a few weeks ago when I told you about Dr. Morrison's daughter who was going to find herself in Nepal for a month?"

I started jumping up and down even before he finished talking. "I got the job, I got the job!"

"Yes, you got the job. Dr. Morrison spoke to the head of the zoology department at the Bolte Museum with the upshot that you will be allowed to fill in for Melissa for the month of August."

I did a very cool victory dance around the room. "I got the job, I got the job."

Brother made a pretend frown. "You're not having some sort of attack, are you? All that jerking of your arms and legs . . . Oh, wait, you're *dancing*."

"Ha, ha." I stopped long enough to whap him on the arm. "So funny I almost laughed up my spleen. I have a job! Coolio!"

One half of his Unibrow rose. "Aren't you even interested in what the job is?"

"Nope. I like animals, so it'll be OK." I started toward the door. "Gotta call Holly and tell her she's not the only one who will be making oodles of money." I paused at the door and looked back. "It does pay great, huge gobs of money, right? 'Cause it's a museum job? I need money, Brother. That allowance you give me is positively minuscule."

"You get a perfectly acceptable allowance—"

"Yeah, it's fine if you don't have a life or anything, but excuse me, I do! I want to go to movies, and buy CDs, and clothes, and makeup, and presents for people, and go to places like London. I'm seventeen, Brother! Money is not just an option when you're seventeen; it's a requirement!"

"You'll find out the pay rate when you go in on Monday," Brother said, his voice tired. I stood there for a minute looking at him. You know, really looking at him. There were black circles under his eyes, and with his hair cut all butch, he looked old. Really old. Older than he was, and we both know he's ancient.

"Are you all right?" I asked, suddenly worried about him.

He looked surprised, rubbing his forehead before answering. "Are you inquiring into my general health or mental state?"

"Brother, we both know your mental state is Froot Loop city," I said, trying to squish down the sick feeling of worry that was boiling up in my stomach. "You don't, like, have cancer or something and you're not telling me because you don't want to ruin my last month in England, the last and greatest month because not only is Dru coming to visit for a couple of days, but Fang will be coming home from New Zealand in a week, and I'll finally be able to pin him down about the whole girl/guy thing? You're not hiding the fact that you're going to croak soon, are you?"

"No," he said, rubbing his head again. "It's not that."

"Oh. Good." I waited a few seconds for him to tell me what the problem was, but he didn't. He just sat there looking old. Part of me wanted to ignore whatever it was, but the other part of me, the really annoying part, had me adding, "I wouldn't like it if you were sick."

He stopped rubbing his head and did that old-guy blink a couple of times. "Thank you, Emily. I know how much that admission must have cost you."

"I'd probably even cry."

He cleared his throat in embarrassment and rubbed the bridge of his nose. "Would you, indeed? I'm very touched. I didn't know you cared."

"Not in front of anyone, though," I figured I'd better add. "Because you know how my nose goes all snot-locker when I cry, and my face turns red, and my mascara runs and stuff. But I'd cry where no one could see me."

He sighed one more time. "No, I guess I couldn't

5

expect you to be snot-lockerish in front of people. Good night, Emily."

"Nighty-night, don't let Mom bite," I said, snickering as I beetled off to my room feeling all warm and fuzzy. Sometimes you have to let the ancient ones know they matter, even when they annoy you to death. Did I tell you that I'm not speaking to Mom? She's trying to get me to start packing now, even though we won't be going home to Seattle until the thirtieth of the month. Like I want to spend my last precious month packing stuff? Gah!

Anyhoo, I'll let you know tomorrow how the new job goes. It's bound to be fun working with animals in a museum, don't you think? I thought I was going to have to end up working at the kids' summer camp with Holly, but woo-hoo, I have a museum job!

How's Felix the cat? What did you guys do this weekend? And are you getting excited about coming to England? It's a real pain in the butt that your mom could only afford one week in Europe, but oh, well, at least we'll be together for three days! I can't wait for you to meet my friends here. I can't wait for you to drool over Fang.

I sure miss him. It's been, like, forever since he went off to work on his cousin's farm.

Tell all about what you're packing!

Hugs and smooches,
~Em

Subject: re: Hippo birdies 2 ewe!
From: Emmers@britsahoy.co.uk
To: fbaxter@ganglia.co.nz
Date: 1 August 2004 10:40pm

Fang wrote:
> *Thank you for the birthday card and wishes. I*
> *spent the day helping my cousin repair a fence that*
> *had been destroyed by cattle from the neighboring*
> *farm, but I appreciated the card and the CD you*
> *made for me. I'll be home on the eighth, so stop*
> *worrying.*

You had to work on your birthday? Sheesh! Oh, well, I suppose that's how they do things there. I'm so happy you'll be home soon! I can't wait to hear all about your summer in NZ . . . no, wait, you said it was winter there, huh? Whatever, I can't wait to hear about it.

I ran into Aidan the other day. He's just as icky as ever, although he didn't go all potty-mouth on me like he has in the past. And he asked where you were, which I thought was nice, and he said he is going to Oxford in the fall, so I guess everything worked out with him transferring schools. He didn't ask about Devon, though. Guess he's still mad about Devon beating him up after we got back from Paris. I know you and Dev had kind of given Aidan up, so I hope you won't be too hurt or anything that he's still a poophead.

There's loads more I have to tell you. It's been really strange with you gone. I wish you had come back in July, like you were going to, but I'm not going to yell at you about that. Aren't you impressed? I've been doing some thinking, Fang, and . . . um . . . never mind. I'll tell you when you get home.

I'm really, *really* glad you're coming back.

Emily

Subject: Want some cheese with that whine?
From: Emmers@britsahoy.co.uk
To: Devonator@skynetcomm.com
Date: 1 August 2004 10:53pm

Devonator wrote:
> *so I won't be back to England for a couple more*
> *weeks. I've got the villa to myself, which is good,*
> *but it would be more fun with you here. Anyway,*
> *can you come out for a few days? My uncle won't*
> *be back from Rome for a few weeks, so it's cool if*
> *you can come. You can even bring Holly, if her*
> *parents will let her go to Greece.*

Man, I'd love to come to Greece, but I just can't. I've got a job starting tomorrow—score! A real job, too, one in a museum and everything! So I can't come, but thank you for asking. I miss you like mad! You may think it's no fun not knowing anyone in Greece, but I know you, Dev—you're a babe magnet. I bet you have girls crawling all over you.

I, on the other hand, am here by my sad and lonesome self. Fang is gone, you are gone, Holly spends most of her weekends on the phone with Ruaraidh, even Bess has been busy, what with her witch training and stuff. My mom is obsessed with packing, and Brother is downright weird.

Anyway, I can't wait for you to come home. You'll be back before I have to go, right? You're my best guy friend, Dev, even if you're not my boyfriend anymore. Any guy who lets me barf on him (twice!) and still wants to hang with me is pretty fabu. I just couldn't leave England without seeing you again.

Hugsies!
Emily

Subject: OH! MY! GOD!!!
From: Emmers@britsahoy.co.uk
To: Dru@seattlegrrl.com
Date: 2 August 2004 6:18pm

So! I went to work today to fill in for the daughter of one of Brother's professor friends while she's off with her BF. I don't think her dad knows about that, BTW, but Evelyn, the girl at the museum café, told me that the girl I'm filling in for went off with her BF because her dad wouldn't let her see him. I'm telling you, it's a big old pain in the patootie to have a medieval scholar for a father. They're so incredibly *old!*

Anyway, I trotted into the museum today like a good little girl, and filled out the papers, etc. and got the scoop on money (we get paid at the end of every week!), then followed the personnel lady to my new job.

"You know, of course, that the Bolte Museum is the finest natural history museum outside of London," the P-lady said as we walked through the museum. It wasn't open yet, which made it really cool to walk by the big windows in the front where a bunch of people were lining up to get in. "In addition, our cultural galleries are very highly respected. But you will, of course, be interested in the natural history departments. As you can see, we have galleries devoted to geology, anthropology and archaeology, botany, and zoology, which includes exhibits on mammals, amphibians, invertebrates, and, of course, the section you will be working in—birds."

I looked around as we walked through the halls of the museum, our footsteps doing that eerie echo thing as we passed big dinosaur skeletons, cases with stuffed animals (but not icky ones like kittens and squirrels like that place in Scotland had), big glass wall cases full of dead butterflies, and other weird stuff. "I get to work with birds? Cool! I have birds. A girl at school had a pair of zebra finches, and she was going to let them go, but that's just wrong, because zebra finches are from Africa. So the birds would die if she dumped them, which of course meant I had to take them. I had to rename them, though, 'cause she'd given them silly names like J-Lo and Ben, and I ask you, who could live with zebra finches named J-Lo and Ben? Now they're Buffy and Spike, which is a whole lot better, don't you think?"

The woman gave me an odd look. "Erm . . . yes. Here we are. This door leads to the ornithology department. It is kept locked at all times. Normally you will use the back entrance, but just this once I'll take you in this way."

She pulled out a bunch of keys and unlocked the dark red door labeled PRIVATE, waving me in ahead of her.

"Wow, behind the scenes at a museum," I said, looking around the big room. Behind me I could see the backs of the glass cases with the butterflies. You could see through to the museum if you bent over and peered out through the butterfly bodies. The room I was in was huge, part of it filled with row after row after row of five-foot-tall, long, really wide cabinets, with offices at either end of the room.   •

"Those offices are for the curators of the respective zoology departments," the personnel lady said as she hustled me to the left, through a maze of the filing cabinets. "You will be working in the ornithology workroom, back here. Helen Bonner will be your immediate supervisor. She is the ornithology collections manager."

"Oh. Cool. Hey, what's in all these filing cabinets?" I tried to read what the labels said on the drawers, but they were written in Latin or Klingon or something.

The P-lady stopped in front of a door. "Birds, of course. Helen, here is your new assistant. I will leave her in your hands."

Birds? In the filing cabinets? That was, like, animal cruelty! They couldn't look out or anything! OMG!

I looked at the last of the cases before going into the small office to meet my boss, planning on telling her that I didn't think it was right at all to keep birds in filing cabinets. How much could it cost them to get proper cages?

"Thank you, Beryl," the woman named Helen said as I looked around. I hadn't realized at first that there was more beyond all the filing cabinets, but in addition to the small room where a nice-looking woman with short, curly hair was standing hugging her coffee cup, there was a room beyond that had a couple of big tables, lots of counters and sinks, and about five refrigerators. I figured it must be the lunchroom.

"Emily Williams, isn't it?" Helen asked, declutching her coffee mug long enough to shake my hand. "I'm so glad to see you. Melissa's sudden holiday has thrown my entire schedule into chaos. Now, let me give you a quick tour, then we'll get you to work, all right?"

"OK," I said, worrying a bit about the birds as we passed the filing cabinets and headed for the rooms the P-lady had said were the curator's. Was it going to be my job to clean up the bottom of the filing cabinet drawers? I had to change the paper in Buffy and Spike's cage every day; otherwise poop built up everywhere. I didn't like thinking about having to clean out all those filing cabinets, but the money was good, and I did have bird experience.

I wanted to stop and peek at the birds, but Helen evidently meant what she said about being behind, because she hurried me past the cabinets and into a small room with a couple of tables and people sitting around them. "This is the vertebrates room. Everyone, this is Emily Williams. She's filling in for Melissa while she's on holiday. That's Sam and Kia there, Brent, Chris Greater and Chris Lesser—that's our little joke to tell which one we're referring—are at the gassing jars, and this is Lars. He's a cultural anthropologist, but we often see him."

I smiled my second-best smile at everyone, and even shook Lars's hand when he grabbed mine (guy check: old and not cute in the least, although his eyes were nice and sparkly).

"I'm just showing Emily about," Helen said as she headed out the opposite end of the room, pausing to grab two white hospital face masks from a bag sitting on a counter. "In here is the beetle room, Emily. Unfortunately, the boiling room is in here as well. Put your mask on. It doesn't keep the smell out entirely, but it will help."

Smell? Boiling room? *Beetle room?* I was starting to wonder just what these people were doing with birds when I put the mask on and followed Helen through the door.

"Close the door," she said, kind of muffled behind the mask. I choked on the smell—I can't even begin to tell you how awful it was! It was like a compost heap or something. It was so bad, it made my eyes water. "Because the beetles will decimate the collection if they get out, we have to make sure the outer door is closed before the door to the beetle room is opened."

The door made a soft, hushed noise as it closed, and I noticed that it had little flap thingies on all the sides, evidently to keep beetles from crawling through it.

Beetles!

"Um. What exactly are the beetles used— Oh, my God!"

Helen had opened the door to a tiny room. In the middle of it stood a tall wooden case almost as tall as she was. The front of the case had about ten drawers. She pulled out one of the drawers and I looked down to see a skeleton of something, some animal covered in little brown beetles.

"These are dermestid beetles. They strip the flesh off the animals and birds very quickly—this is a bat. Down here . . . ah, yes, here we have a couple of our specimens."

14

She pulled open another drawer, which was filled with dead birds swarmed with more beetles. I just stared at them, wondering what sort of horrible people would feed birds and bats to beetles. Were they all insane?

"Why?" I finally managed to gasp (it was almost a gag, because let me tell you, the smell of beetles eating dead things is grottier than grotty. In fact, it's pretty much the king of grotty).

"The beetles are very efficient. They strip most birds in a matter of days. The larger mammals take longer, but even they can be stripped down to their skeleton in a week."

I stared at her in horror, the hair on the back of my neck standing on end. "Skeletons?"

"Yes, skeletons. The skins, of course, are removed before the carcass is fed to the beetles."

"Of course," I said, wondering if it was a good idea to go insane right at that moment, or wait until I was away from the beetles. I rubbed my arms, feeling all creepy, like beetles were crawling on me.

"You can see why it's very important that we be careful with the beetles," she said as she pushed the drawer closed. "I would hate to think of what would happen if they were to get into the collection."

"Uh," I said, which honestly was about all I could say without screaming and running like mad from the Room of Beetle Horrors.

"If you go back through the door . . . there you are.

Over here are the boiling kettles." She had to yell because we were walking away from the beetle room and into what looked like a small lab where a really loud exhaust fan was running. It was like having a jet engine blasting away in the same room. "Those are for the mammal department. We don't boil the bird skeletons. We find that if we allow them to soak in plain tap water for a week or so, the bacteria in the water does an excellent job of soaking and loosening the ligaments and tendons that the beetles didn't get."

She waved her hand at a row of big tall glass jars that lined one of the counters. In each one were a handful of bones. Bird bones, I assumed, but even so, it was totally freaky.

"Why do you want bird skeletons?" I yelled, breathing through my mouth because it stank *so bad* in that room that I wanted to ralph right then and there.

She tipped her head to the side. "Why do we want skeletons?"

"Yeah! Why?"

She blinked a couple of times, then said, "Emily, the Bolte Museum has one of the finest collections of bird and mammal skins and skeletons in England. Students come from Oxford and other universities to study the specimens."

My skin crawled as I looked around the room, suddenly understanding why they kept birds in the filing cabinets. They were dead birds! *Dead!* "You mean everything you have here is *dead?*"

16

"Yes, of course! Your job is to clean the bird skeletons, then number the bones so they can be put into service for zoologists and students."

"And everyone here—those people out there, the two Chrises and everyone—they're all doing things to dead animals?"

She looked at me like I was the one who was a pimento short of an olive loaf. "Yes, Emily. This is a natural history museum. Our collections are noted throughout the world."

I clutched the counter for a minute, thinking seriously about fainting, but who knew what these weirdos would do to me if I did—they'd probably feed me to the beetles!

"Come along. We have much to see. I have a practice set of bones I'd like you to label. You can write very small, can't you?"

As I left the torture chamber, I looked behind me at the horrible bones in water, at the five huge metal spaghetti kettles simmering gently along a side counter, and the door to the beetle room. Those bratty kids at Holly's summer camp were starting to look better and better. "Yeah, I can write small."

"Excellent. Once you do that, you can get started cleaning the bones. There's quite a backlog since Melissa left, but I'm sure you'll get through it in no time."

"That's assuming I don't either get eaten by beetles, or am carted away by the folks at the loony bin,"

17

I said with a majorly creeped-out shiver as we walked past the filing cabinets toward her office.

"What was that?" she asked, pausing to wait for me to catch up.

"Nothing."

The rest of the morning was just as freaky, Dru. I kid you not—this whole museum is made up of dead things! I peeked into one of the filing cabinets before lunch, and it had a bunch of stuffed birds in it!

The dry bones weren't too bad, though. They were kind of interesting, once you got over the fact that they were some poor little birdie's bones. The practice skeleton Helen had me working on was for a sparrow, and each teeny, tiny little bone had to be numbered. They had these special really fine-point pens, and I had a skeleton guide that showed me how to number each bone. It was pretty cool, and I only screwed up half a dozen times. Thank God for Wite-Out!

So here I am, Emily the bird-skeleton girl. I would quit the job except for two things: I really need the money (I have to have money for when you're here so we can go out and do all sorts of fun stuff), and a museum job will look good on my résumé. Plus Helen reassured me that I won't have to see the dead birds until they've been beetled, and I have to admit, they don't look very birdlike after the beetles get through with them. So I guess since I won't have to see actual dead bird bodies, and won't have to do anything with the beetles (Helen said she does that), I'll stay.

How come you didn't e-mail me about your weekend with Felix? You're obligated by law to tell me *everything!* So dish, girl!

Hugs and kisses,
~Em

Subject: re: You're *SO* not going to believe this!!!!!!!
From: Emmers@britsahoy.co.uk
To: Dru@seattlegrrl.com
Date: 3 August 2004 9:40pm

Dru wrote:
> *and then after dinner, we went to see* Catwoman
> *(have you seen it yet? It's totally cheese on*
> *toast!), and after that, we were sitting in Felix's*
> *car, and he said he loved me, and I said that I*
> *loved him too, and then, OMG!!! He asked me*
> *to marry him! And I said I would!!!! I'm*
> *ENGAGED!!!!!!!!!!!!!!!!!!!!!!!!!!!!!!!*

No! You are not! *No!* Omigod! Dru! You're engaged? You're going to get married? You're only seventeen! OMG, you've given me a case of the screaming fantods! *You're getting married!*

OK, back. I had to go tell Mom and call Holly. Mom said that she hopes it's going to be a long engagement, and Holly said she thought that was very romantic, and what kind of wedding dress are you going to have?

MARRIED?????

thud

Tell . . . me . . . everything!

Hugs and excited kissies,
~Em

P.S. Mrs. Dru Jackson—that sounds so Hollywood!

Subject: re: You're *SO* not going to believe
           this!!!!!!!
From: Emmers@britsahoy.co.uk
To: Dru@seattlegrrl.com
Date: 3 August 2004 9:42pm

I can't believe you're *engaged!* I mean, that's so . . . wow! *Married!*

~Em the totally stunned

Subject: re: You're *SO* not going to believe
          this!!!!!!!
From: Emmers@britsahoy.co.uk
To: Dru@seattlegrrl.com
Date: 3 August 2004 9:43pm

OK, I got it now! That was a joke, wasn't it? Admit it.
You were pulling my leg. Hahahahahah, I knew it all
along. It was a joke.
　It was, wasn't it?

~Em

Subject: re: Would I do that to you? Fwah!
From: Emmers@britsahoy.co.uk
To: Dru@seattlegrrl.com
Date: 4 August 2004 7:17am

Dru wrote:
> *Silly! It's not a joke! It's all real!!! I'm engaged to*
> *Felix Jackson!!!!!! I haven't told my mom yet,*
> *though, because you know her—she'll have a major*
> *freak attack. And I don't want her to say we can't*
> *go to Europe and see you in a couple of weeks, so*
> *I'm going to tell her when we get home. So tell your*
> *mom it's a secret and make her swear she won't tell*
> *my mom.*

Oh, come on, it's a joke! I've sussed you, chicky! It's
all just a joke that you're pulling, and when you get

here, you'll laugh and laugh and laugh at me because it's all a joke and I fell for it, only I didn't! So there, nyah!

> *Felix is going to go to Washington State University,*
> *but he says they have married students' apartments,*
> *so maybe we'll live there. Only that'll mean I have to*
> *go to Wazu, too, and you know I want to go to*
> *Berkeley! Felix says we'll wait until January, when I*
> *turn eighteen, and then go to Reno or Vegas and*
> *get married. Isn't that romantic? You'll come with*
> *us, won't you? I couldn't get married without my*
> *best friend there!*

Oh. My. God. It's not a joke, is it? You're serious? You're really engaged to Felix? Dru—he's got his nipples pierced! What kind of a guy sticks pins in his nipples, and do you really want to spend the rest of your life with him? I mean, sheesh! What if he wants *you* to get your nipples pierced? That's just wrong! And you know, I heard from Bess that some guys have other stuff pierced, too; *guy* stuff. What if he has a pierced weenus? The *ew* factor on that is way past Gag Town and into Spewsville!

I don't know what to say, Dru. If you really, really, really love him, then I'm happy for you, because you're my best friend and I want you to be really, really, really in love with a guy who's in love with you, but crikey! You'd give up the University of California for him? I know he's nice and all, but is he nice enough to give up *Berkeley?*

What about us? What will happen to me if you get married? We were going to meet in Chicago during vacations and stuff—you coming from Berkeley, and me from Harvard. We were going to go to all the swishy stores, and see loads of movies, and order room service so we can have chocolate martinis in our hotel room, and now we won't be able to do that! *Wah!*

That sounds selfish, doesn't it? I'm sorry. I don't mean to be selfish. But damn, girl! You'd give up *everything* for Felix?

E-mail me as soon as you get up.

Hugs and worried kisses,
~Em

Subject: re: Now you're making me cry
From: Emmers@britsahoy.co.uk
To: Dru@seattlegrrl.com
Date: 4 August 2004 5:35pm

Dru wrote:
> *and then Mom came in and saw me crying, and I*
> *had to lie to her and say that you told me some-*
> *thing sad, and not that I felt so bad about not being*

23

> able to meet you in Chicago like we planned. But
> don't worry, just because I'm marrying Felix doesn't
> mean we can't still do the Chicago thing. We'll have
> martinis in the hotel room, and dance around
> fountains, and see shows and stuff. I'll just be
> married, that's all! Besides, we probably won't get
> married until January.

January is a long way off, isn't it? Four months. A lot can happen in four months. Guys can go totally butt-wipe in four months. I'm sorry I made you cry, but it was just kind of a shock. You know I'm really happy for you, right?

So, my day was . . . um . . . odd. First of all, I found out that the people who were hanging around outside of the beetle room also work outside of the office that I share with Helen and Wynn. He's the bird curator, but according to Chris Lesser—she's the younger Chris, the older one being a guy who looks just like Rupert Everett—more about him in a mo . . . anyway, according to CL, Wynn is never there. Get this—he's always out on hunting trips! *Hunting!* That's how they get all the birds to feed to the beetles! OMG!

"They go out and shoot birds?" I asked at lunch.

CL nodded. "Yes. It's for research, of course."

"But the research is for stuff like bird protection and things, right?"

She nodded again, dabbing at her mouth with a napkin. "A good deal of the researchers using the collection are interested in the impact birds have on their environment, as well as how various environmental issues are affecting birdlife in the UK."

I waved my chicken gyro at her. "But they go out and *kill* birds first?"

"Yes, I just said so." She set down her hamburger and frowned at me. "Research is a very important part of the Bolte Museum."

"Yeah, but don't you think that killing the birds to see what sort of impact they have is a little, like, crazy? Can't people just go out and watch them instead of shooting them?"

"But then we wouldn't be able to know everything there is to know about the birds, would we?" CL asked in kind of a snotty tone.

I let that go because obviously she was part of a deranged group of people who thought killing birds was the only way to study them.

"Who's up for a party next Friday?" Chris Greater (aka Mr. Nummy) asked as he plopped his plate down at the tiny little café table CL and I were sitting at. Behind him were Brent, Kia, and Sam (who is a girl, not a guy). Her name is actually Samia, and she's Pakistani, but everyone calls her Sam. The last three grabbed another of the tables and hauled it up to ours, so we could all sit together. I think Kia and Brent are going together—they both brought their lunches in the same sort of insulated lunch bags, and Kia stole some of Brent's grapes without him saying anything. Everyone else bought lunch at the café, which was pretty good. They have lots of vegetarian food, and also make lattes. Civilization at last!

"A party?" CL asked, dribbling a bit of mustard down her chin. "Next Friday? I'm good for it."

"That's Friday the thirteenth," Brent pointed out.

"I can do Friday as well," Sam said. She looked at me and smiled. "How about you, Emily? You want to join us?"

"Sure," I said, more than a little bit relieved that someone had asked me, so I wouldn't have to act like I didn't want to go. "What time is it?"

Sam turned back to CG. "Before or after lunch?"

"Oh, before, don't you think?" he asked as he smiled at me. A smile! From a hottie! A university grad student hottie! Grad students are worth, like, a hundred points, aren't they? And he was asking me when to have the party? Yes! The Emily magic touch is back!

"Before, sure, that sounds *über*-fabu," I said with much coolness. If there's one thing I've learned living here, it's that the Brits don't jump up and down and get excited about stuff unless it's one of their soccer games. Then they go totally Springer.

"That's settled, then," CG said. Brent asked something about getting a permit to go hunt some poor, innocent animal, and I spent a bit of time watching CG to give him the Hottie Objective Response Exam, aka HORE (snort, giggle. Hore? Get it? Sounds like . . . ? Hoot!).

Like I said, Chris the guy looked a lot like Rupert Everett. He had curly dark hair and gray eyes, and a bit of manly stubble (you know how stubble sends me! Must remember to talk stubble with Fang when he gets back), and he wore very tight T-shirts. I liked him, and would have thought seriously about going after him, but you know the plan: the minute Fang comes back from his trip to New Zealand, I'm going to tackle this whole Fang/Emily thing. Yeah, yeah, I know you said I should have done it when I got back from Paris, but I couldn't because he was just leaving for NZ.

I really am cheesed off at his cousin sending him a ticket out of the blue like that. If he hadn't, Fang would have been here the whole summer, and I would have had time to do some serious girlfriending by now! Instead I'm going to have to fit it all into only four weeks, not to mention figure out a way to get Fang to come home with us.

How did I get on that subject? Oh, yeah, I was doing the HORE thing. Anyhoo, I liked CG, but I won't be seducing him because my heart belongs to Fang. I think. Maybe. If he wants it. You think he does, right? He's e-mailed me every couple of days, and not even Devon e-mails me that much!

No. I'm being silly. Fang wants me. Everyone says he does. He just couldn't turn down a free trip to New Zealand, that's all.

The rest of lunch was OK. Everyone wanted to know how I ended up in England, and where I was going to go to college, and stuff like that. Then they told me about the ghost.

Yes, ghost. Only in England does everything have ghosts attached to it!

"Just don't work too late," Brent said, making googly eyes at everyone. "You don't want to be in the museum alone late at night."

Kia giggled. CL rolled her eyes as she pulled out one of those little foil packets of wet hand wipes and wiped off her hamburgery hands. "Must we go into that bit of foolishness again?"

CG grinned, and said in a really loud whisper, "Odd things happen here at night."

"The building is haunted," Sam said in a matter-of-fact tone.

"It is not haunted. That's just a stupid rumor put 'round by one of the janitors. Ignore them, Emily. They like to let their imaginations run away with them."

"Oh, I know woo-woo," I answered. "It doesn't scare me—I have a ghost in my bedroom. In my underwear drawer, really. It's been on vacation or something for the last month, but I know it'll come back. It always comes back just when I think it's finally gone."

Everyone stared at me like I had turned into a giant

pumpkin or something. "You have a ghost in your underwear drawer?" Kia finally asked.

"Yup. It likes to fondle my bras, which is just too pervy for words. But I'm going to get rid of it. My sister has been at Wiccan school since June, and she's going to conduct an exorcism to get rid of the ghost for good as soon as she comes home."

"Haunted Alans," CG said, looking at Brent. "That's a new one, innit?"

Brent waggled his eyebrows.

"Alans?" I asked.

"Alan Whickers," CG said, grinning at me again.

"Uh . . ."

"It's rhyming slang. You've heard of that, yes?" CL asked. I nodded. Rhyming slang was something they did a lot in London a long time ago. Evidently some people still use it. It's like *so* yesterday. "Alan Whickers means knickers. Sometimes people just say Alans."

And now you know why I am not worried about my undie ghost ever hurting me. How could a ghost from a country that called undies Alan Whickers be harmful?

"OK. Gotcha. Alans." What*ever!*

Brent snapped the end off a pickle and asked (while he was eating it, which is just gross with a capital gah!), "So you wouldn't be afraid of the ghost of Henpecked Harry if you ran into him, Emily?"

"Henpecked Harry?"

"That's the name of the man who originally owned this land," Sam said, nibbling on a piece of celery stuffed with cream cheese. "Sir Harry Bolte. The museum used to be housed in Bolte House, but that was destroyed in World War Two."

"When they tore down the old house, they found a skeleton sealed up in a wall," Brent said in a hushed voice. I couldn't tell if he was trying to freak me out, or if he was really scared of the ghost. "They said the scratch marks where the poor devil tried to claw his way through the wood were still visible."

"You're talking cack," CL said. "There is *no* ghost. Emily, don't listen to them; they just like to mix things up."

"We don't want her to be scared," Brent said with a really innocent look on his face. I figured he must be trying to pull a fast one on me then, because no one looks that innocent!

"So why do they call the ghost Henpecked Harry?" I asked, just to be polite.

"Rumor has it that it was Sir Harry's wife who had him sealed up in the walls. She was a right trollop, you know."

"She was?"

"Oh, yeah. Used to play army with all the blokes on the estate."

"Army?" I asked, almost wishing I hadn't because I just knew the answer was going to be stupid.

Brent leaned even closer so he could whisper in my

ear. Kia didn't look too happy about that. "You know, *army*. It's where a guy lies down and his bird—"

"Brent, stop being such an arse," CL interrupted.

I rubbed my ear where Brent had breathed on it. Obviously he was the kind of guy who thought saying something like that to girls was amusing. In other words, he was an Aidan. Blech! Like I need another one of those in my life?

"I'm not afraid of ghosts," I said, ignoring Brent. "So you don't have to worry about me."

"There is no ghost," CL repeated, glaring at Brent.

"I've seen it," Sam said, taking a swig of power water.

"You didn't!" CL argued.

"Yes, I did. Saw it last year. Around Samhain, wasn't it?" She tipped her head at Chris G. "You remember—I told you the next day I'd seen the ghost."

"That's right. You said he was near the freezers and he floated right through the window when he saw you."

"Made an awful mess, he did," Sam said, closing the lid to her water bottle. She gathered up her tray and took it over to a nearby tray dump. "Took me half the night to clean up the shambles he'd left in the skinning room. I'm off for a lie in the sun. Anyone coming with?"

"I will," Kia said, grabbing her sandwich and shooting Brent a warning look.

"Well, it doesn't matter, I'm very cool with ghosts,"

I said, doing a quick tongue-on-the-teeth check to make sure I didn't have bits of gyro stuck anywhere before I smiled at hottie Chris. "And I love parties!"

"Good, we'll put you down for Friday."

The rest of the day was pretty normal, if you can call numbering bird skeletons *normal*. Thank God this job is just for a month! Bess is going to have kittens when she comes back from Wiccan school and finds out I'm working for bird killers!

Oh! Speaking of birds, I forgot to tell you that Buffy and Spike had a baby! How cool is that? You know how Buffy is always laying eggs and then after a few days she gets off the nest 'cause she's bored? Well, I've been kind of busy the last few weeks, and didn't notice that one of the eggs actually hatched! There's a really ugly, teeny tiny baby with a gigantic head in the nest. We're talking majorly ugly. But now I have to think of a name for him. You'll help me, right? You're good with names. Of course, there was that time a few months ago when you tried to get your mom to legally change your name to Esmeralda because you thought it was too Goth for words (it wasn't), but I'm willing to overlook that bit of temporary insanity.

Gotta run; it's din-din time and I have to see what's up with Brother. He's been acting odd lately. He hasn't yelled at me for using the phone, or hogging the computer, and he didn't even come unglued when he found out that I drove Mom's car to the store (stupid English law says I can't, but honestly, I've been driving

for almost two years now! And I drove in Scotland!).
In other words, Brother has turned normal, and I want
to know why.

You still haven't told me everything about the date
with Felix. I want all the details!

Hugs and kissy-poos,
~Em

Subject: I hate this!
From: Emmers@britsahoy.co.uk
To: Dru@seattlegrrl.com
Date: 6 August 2004 8:31pm

Brother has leprosy or the black plague or the pox or
something, I just know he does. He's walking around
looking all gray and old and he's *not eating!* Have you
ever known my father to pass up food? That's proof
that something is wrong.

"Mom, we need to have a talk about Brother," I
said this afternoon as soon as I came home from
shopping. (I got paid today—have I mentioned how
nice it is to be paid in cash?—and of course that
meant I had to go buy clothes.)

"Mmm?" Mom said, frowning at a box of stuff she
was packing. "I wonder if I shouldn't wrap my relish
dishes in towels, instead of newspaper? It would
mean unpacking the towel box, but that couldn't
hurt, could it?"

"Only if you're borderline obsessed with towels, like someone I could mention," I said darkly, but she missed the hint and just looked at me like I was disturbing her or something.

"What is it you want, Emily?"

"I want to know what's up with Brother. Why didn't he eat dinner tonight?"

"Probably because he wasn't hungry." She held up one of the ceramic relish trays she had painted with scenes from the Domesday Book (really old book that's supposed to be important, although honestly, the drawings in it look like they were made by a cat on Valium). "Perhaps if I were to get some of that bubble wrap . . ."

"Hel-*lo!*" I waved my arms in front of her. "We're talking about my father here, your husband, the man you bound us all to without first finding out if his family had a history of cancer or dysentery or anything like that. Haven't you noticed that something is wrong with him?"

"Wrong with who, dear?" Mom asked, eyeing another relish tray (for some reason all she ended up painting on were relish trays, so now we have cornered the entire western hemisphere's relish tray market).

"Brother!"

She looked up at that. "What's wrong with him?"

"That's what I'm asking you!" I all but yelled. Honestly! Parents!

"There's nothing wrong with him, Em. He's just tired from trying to finish his research before we have to leave. What do you think—bubble wrap, towels, or some of those horrible white Styrofoam packing peanuts?"

"*Argh!*" I yelled, frustrated and all that jazz. Brother won't tell me anything; he just looks sad when I ask him what's wrong, and shakes his head. Mom is obviously in la-la land. Bess isn't due back until Monday. Clearly I'm going to have to get to the bottom of the situation myself, since there's no one else sane in my family. I told Mom that, but she just said, "That's nice, Em," and asked me if I thought real popcorn would do as a packing substance.

I *argh*ed again and went off to my room to see how Buffy and Spike and the baby were.

I thought about your suggestion of Giles, but decided to name him Beaky because he was born with a birth defect—he's got no upper beak. I'm not sure why, and it makes his head look a little weird, but he's still kind of cute in an ugly-baby-bird-missing-part-of-his-beak way.

Sunday is Fang day! Must go to plan out the perfect outfit. Tell me how the dinner with your grandma goes. I'm betting she drops her teeth right onto the dinner plate when you tell her you're getting married!

Hugsies and one-beaked smooches,
~Emily

Subject: re: Which says GF more—chinos or a silk and
         lace cami?
From: Emmers@britsahoy.co.uk
To: Devonator@skynetcomm.com
Date: 7 August 2004 11:02am

Devonator wrote:
> *doesn't matter at all what you wear; Fang will be*
> *happy just to see you. I appreciate you sending me*
> *pictures of all your clothes so I can help you pick out*
> *what to wear to see him, but you filled up my inbox*
> *and the ISP screamed. I thought you asked Holly*
> *what you should wear to things? Isn't that a girl*
> *thing?*

I'm an equal-opportunity friend, and besides, Holly's
been at the day camp every day, and she's busy at
home because her mom broke her leg and Holly has
to cook dinner and stuff. Her brother is coming
home next week, so she should be able to help me
with major fashion decisions then, but Fang will be
here *tomorrow!* I figured you as Mr. Player and an
ex-BF should be able to tell me what constitutes potential GF wear, and what just looks like a friend. I
don't have any time to waste, Devon. I have to go
straight into GF-hood or else!

Sorry to hear you had the uglies. Don't drink the

water again! Mom says boiled rice should help.

Hugs,
Emily

Subject: Welcome to MyLifeIsOver.com
From: Emmers@britsahoy.co.uk
To: Dru@seattlegrrl.com
Date: 8 August 2004 6:15pm

That's it. I'm officially giving up on life. I'm going to become a hermit.

Just thought you'd like to know.

~Em the heartbroken

Subject: Life as I know it is over
From: Emmers@britsahoy.co.uk
To: Devonator@skynetcomm.com
Date: 7 August 2004 6:24pm

I've changed my mind. I'm coming to Greece.

Sobbingly,
Emily

37

Subject: Enquiry via *Teenwise* health form
From: Emmers@britsahoy.co.uk
To: DrAnnaKnows@teenwise.healthsavvy.co.uk
Date: 8 August 2004 6:33pm

Hi, Dr. Anna, I have a question about whether or not it's possible to actually die of a broken heart. I feel sick to my stomach and am kind of dizzy, and I think I'm seeing spots and stuff before my eyes. Does that sound fatal to you? Could you e-mail me back if those are the symptoms of imminent death?

Thanks.
Emily Williams

Subject: re: Welcome to MyLifeIsOver.com
From: Emmers@britsahoy.co.uk
To: Dru@seattlegrrl.com
Date: 8 August 2004 6:49pm

Dru wrote:
> *What's wrong? Em? Why are you going to become*
> *a hermit? Is it something to do with Fang? Didn't he*
> *like the pleated mini and your silk cami? How could*
> *he not like that? It so totally rocks on toast!*

Of course it's something to do with Fang! Would my life be over for just anything?

Oh, great. I think I'm having a heart palpitation. I

don't even know what they are and now I'm having them! It's all Fang's fault, too. I just hope he'll be happy when they find my cold, lifeless body. Maybe I ought to put on my slinky black Diane von Furstenberg dress so I can be buried in it.

I wonder if it's against hermit rules to wear Diane von Furstenberg?

Hugs and kisses (not that I feel like sharing them, but I will because I'm now Saint Emily the Hermit. Plus you haven't done anything wrong, and your heart isn't breaking),

~Em

Subject: re: WHAT!!! IS!!! WRONG???!!!
From: Emmers@britsahoy.co.uk
To: Dru@seattlegrrl.com
Date: 8 August 2004 7:49pm

Dru wrote:
> Come on, Em—spill! You made me tell you
> everything when Tim dumped me (I still can't
> believe no one told me he was only using me
> because he was crushing on my mom!), so now you
> have to spill with the horrors. Did Fang tell you he
> didn't like what you were wearing or something?

No, it wasn't that.

> *You were wearing the forest-green cami, right? And*
> *the moss-green pleated mini? The one that looks so*
> *Beyoncé?*

Yes, I was wearing that, and no, it wasn't the clothes (I bought the coolest go-go boots to go with the mini—they have hearts all over the heels!).

> *Because if you were wearing that peach cami that*
> *you bought last year, then I could understand the*
> *problem. I'm your best friend, Em, so it's up to me*
> *to tell you peach makes you look like you're going*
> *to ralph. But green on you is totally fabu! So if you*
> *wore the green, go you, and if you wore the peach*
> *and Fang dumped you because you looked like you*
> *were going to barf, well, I told you so.*

WILL YOU STOP GOING ON ABOUT CLOTHES?!? It's not the clothes! I looked great! I looked *über*-fabu! I looked *über-über*-fabu! It isn't that at all! (And I do not look like I'm going to barf in peach! That's just a lie!)

Oh, I might as well tell you the whole horrible thing. I have nothing else to do but wait for the woman from the teen crisis place to let me know if I'm about to keel over or not. Did I tell you I'm seeing spots?

The day started out OK. I took the train to the airport with Holly. She got a neighbor in to sit with her mom so she could come with me, and we decided that since Fang's flight didn't come in until after lunch, we'd have a girl's day and do shopping, lunch, etc. So we zoomed into London really early in the morning, hung around the Virgin store for a while, tried on really expensive clothes at shops in Covent Garden (it's like a mall only with very ritzy shops); then we went out to Heathrow to have lunch while we watched airplanes come in.

"What do you think, should I be, like, all cool and distant when he comes out of customs, or should I throw myself into his arms and snog him like mad?" I asked Holly once we were finished with lunch. We were sitting in the waiting area watching people come through from the customs area. A couple of people waiting had brought flowers for someone, which made me feel bad. I should have thought of flowers! Then again, maybe Fang would think that was too girly.

Holly looked thoughtful as she knitted Ruaraidh yet another sweater. (The guy has about thirty of them now. I think Holly is addicted to knitting, to be honest. She doesn't seem to be able to stop. I'm going to have to look into a knitting twelve-step program for her before I have to leave.) "Oh, Em, I'm not sure. I'd say snog him, but you haven't really snogged him before, have you? And it's hard to kiss a guy the first time because you have to figure out where your nose goes, and which way he's going to tip his head, and all that."

"Good point," I said, a little relieved, to be honest. I got all warm and funny inside whenever I thought about kissing Fang, and I wasn't sure I wanted to do that in public. I mean, what if our faces were in the wrong position when I locked lips with him? I could draw blood or something! That would be too hideous for words. "Although I'd like to point out that he did kiss me once, so it's not like we haven't really done the lip thing. So you think I should be cool and so-phisticated? I like that. I can be sophisticated. Look, how's this?"

I got up and stood next to a wall, taking an Audrey Hepburn in *Breakfast at Tiffany's* pose with one hand wrapped around my waist, the elbow of my other arm resting on my hand. I allowed just the corners of my mouth to curl up in an *über*-sophisticated smile that said, "you want me, but you can't have me."

"Erm," Holly said, her brow wrinkling as she stared at me. "What are you doing with your hand?"

"Pretending I'm holding a cigarette, of course!"

"But you don't smoke."

I rolled my eyes. Just a little bit, so I didn't mess up my smoky topaz eye shadow and lapis mascara that really made my eyes stand out. "It's pretend, silly! I'm being Holly Golightly. She's totally sophisticated."

"Who?"

"Holly Golightly. You know, from *Breffy at Tiffany's*? Audrey Hepburn in very cool retro clothes? I wish I had one of those big black hats and black gloves like she wore. That look is just so tight."

"Why are you trying to be Audrey Hepburn?" Holly asked, her knitting forgotten as she stared at me. "She's dead!"

"Well, I know *that*," I said, de-posing myself to sit next to her. "It was a sophisticated pose. Maybe sophisticated isn't Fang. He not snobbish at all, and he's always telling me to be myself."

Holly nodded. "That's good advice."

"It would be if I knew what exactly that meant. Hey, does that sign say that the flight from New Zealand is in?"

We hung around the door waiting for people to get their luggage, pass through customs, and emerge into the waiting area. I double-checked my lipstick, practiced my best smile (the one where I let my eyes sparkle), and asked Holly if she didn't think I had dimples if I smiled really hard.

"No, I think you just look kind of frightening, like you're thinking about roasting children," she said. I looked in the mirror at my dimple smile. She was right. I looked like I was anticipating a nice chunk of roast kid with a side of kitten jelly.

I was just about to try my "shy Di" smile on her (head down, tipped slightly to the side, peering up through my eyelashes while blushing delicately) when a group of people pushed through the door. In the middle of them was Fang, my Fang, my adorable, puppy-dog-eyed Fang. He'd let his hair grow, so it was brushing his shoulders.

"Ohmigod, ohmigod, ohmigod," I said, my hands starting to shake as I looked at him. He was so gorgeous! So wonderful! So . . . Fang! "I think I'm going to puke!"

"No, you're not," Holly said in a firm voice, smiling as she shoved me forward, toward where Fang was setting down his bag so he could peel off his jacket. "You're going to go over and welcome him back to England."

"Yeah," I said on a long breath. "Welcome to England."

Holly pushed me again and I started to walk toward Fang, who hadn't seen me yet . . . started walking, but by the time I made it across the room, dodging all the other people greeting new arrivals, I was running. Sophisticated, schmophisticated, I was so happy to see him, I had to kiss him or I'd burst.

"Fang!" I yelled just before I got to him. He half-turned toward me, his eyes wide as I launched myself at him. Honest to Pete, Dru, I should be on a track team, because the long jump I did that ended up with me crashing into Fang had to be at least ten feet!

Unfortunately, Fang wasn't expecting for anyone to be long-jumping onto him, so when I threw myself on his chest, he staggered backward, tripped over the bag he'd set down, and crashed onto the ground. I was still clutching him, so I went down as well, and cracked my head on his chin.

That didn't stop me from kissing him, though. Holly said later that my butt wasn't showing or anything, but to be honest, I didn't even care at that moment that I was lying on top of Fang in a public airport in a mini skirt, kissing the guy I wanted to be my BF more than anything. Nope, all I cared about was that Fang was home, and he was mine, and now we could get down to the business of being madly in love with each other. So I kissed his lips and his chin and his cheeks and his eyes and told him how happy I was to see him in-between kisses. He just kind of groaned at first, rubbing the back of his head where it hit the floor, but finally he stopped blinking and squinted at me.

"Emily?"

"Hi," I said, and kissed him alongside his mouth, just to let him know I was happy to see him, but not so slutty that I had to knock him down just to kiss him. You know, it never looks cool to appear *too* eager.

"Emily—" He did the blinky thing a couple more times.

"I'm so happy you're home! You didn't hit your head hard, did you? Sorry about that; I didn't think you were going to fall. Here, let me get off you; then Holly and I will take your bags so you don't make your head worse. Are you surprised to see me? We planned this months ago. Holly's here, too, did I tell you? Oh, Fang, I'm so glad you're home! I've got so much to tell you!"

I got to my feet and was just about to hold my hand out to help Fang—who was still looking a bit dazed—to his feet, when someone else's hand appeared in front of him.

"Hullo," the girl who belonged to the hand said as Fang took it and got to his feet, wincing as he felt his head. She smiled at me as she brushed Fang off. "I'm Audrey, Fang's girlfriend. You must be Emily."

Oh, crap. I have to go get more Kleenex. I'll . . . oh, I don't know when I'll be back. I'm so miserable, Dru, I just want to live in a cave for the rest of my life.

Em

Subject: re: Life as I know it is over
From: Emmers@britsahoy.co.uk
To: Devonator@skynetcomm.com
Date: 8 August 2004 11:19pm

Devonator wrote:
> *What's the matter, love? Things not go well with*
> *Fang? Tell Uncle Dev everything. Seriously, Em, if I*
> *can help, I will. You know Fang's my best mate, and*
> *you'll always be my girl. You know I love you (like a*
> *friend, of course, since that other thing didn't work*
> *out).*

Brother says he won't advance me the money to go to Greece, so I have to stay home. He'll be sorry when I die.

I love you, too, Devon. I wish you were here. Everything is awful. I'm going to become a hermit. Or maybe a nun—one of those women who helps others because she's suffered a lost love.

I'm sorry, I have to go. It's too hard to cry and type at the same time.

Fang didn't wait for me. He's in love with someone else.

Emily

Subject: re: *No!!!*
From: Emmers@britsahoy.co.uk
To: Dru@seattlegrrl.com
Date: 8 August 2004 11:22pm

Dru wrote:
> *OMIGOD! Oh. My. God! He has a girlfriend? Are*
> *you sure? She actually said the word? Maybe you*
> *had a concussion from smacking your head on*
> *Fang's chin? Maybe you hallucinated the whole*
> *thing? Oh, Em! Not a girlfriend?*

Yes. A girlfriend. She's a cousin of the cousin he went to stay with in New Zealand. Her name is Audrey, and she's twenty-one, pretty, and has come to visit her English relatives for a couple of months.

I hate her. I *hate* her! She stole my Fang! He . . . he . . . oh, God, Dru, he doesn't want me! He doesn't love me! He didn't wait for me! He chose *her* instead!

I'm going back to bed. I think the spots before my eyes are worse. My head feels like it's going to explode.

I just want to crawl under the covers and never come out.

Emily

Subject: Can I leave Earth now?
From: Emmers@britsahoy.co.uk
To: Dru@seattlegrrl.com
Date: 9 August 2004 7:53am

The underwear ghost is back. Like I need this right now?

Em, the hermit/nun/ghost magnet/miserable and pathetic excuse for a human

Subject: re: Help!
From: Emmers@britsahoy.co.uk
To: Timandra@ewecomm.com
Date: 10 August 2004 6.55pm

Timandra wrote:
> *know what I can do to help, Emily. You seem to*

> *think I'm a veritable font of wisdom and aid but I'm*
> *afraid about this, I just can't help you. The problem*
> *is that I don't see how sending a metric ton of*
> *sheep manure to this girl's house would help the*
> *situation. If there's anything else I can do, though,*
> *be sure to let me know.*

Oh, never mind. She's staying with her aunt, and it probably wouldn't be fair to mess up her apartment just to annoy Audrey.

Life sucks. You're still a good aunt even if you won't send me sheep poop, although honestly, you live on a sheep farm, I'd think you'd want to get rid of some of it!

Emily

Subject: re: EMILY ANSWER ME RIGHT NOW!!!!
From: Emmers@britsahoy.co.uk
To: Dru@seattlegrrl.com
Date: 10 August 2004 7:13pm

Dru wrote:
> *If you do not e-mail me right this minute I swear to*
> *you, I'm not coming to England! You can't just*
> *disappear for a whole day after such a horrible*
> *blow! Em, please, please, please let me know*
> *you're OK. I'm so worried I couldn't even enjoy*
> *Sukie's face when she saw my ring!*

You have a ring? Felix the Cat got you a ring? With diamonds and everything? A real ring, not just a friendship ring?

I bet it's pretty. You'll have to let me see it when you come next week, because I will never ever have one myself, so I'll have to enjoy yours. In fact, I'm never going to be in love again, or be engaged, or get married, or have kids, or any of that, but you will, so you have to promise that you'll let me live whatchamacallit through you. Vicariously. I'll just live vicariously through you, OK?

> *What did you do after that she-witch grabbed*
> *Fang? What did he say? Did he look embarrassed?*

I stood there. Nothing. Yes. Happy now? You're making me relive everything, and you as my BFF are supposed to tell me I don't need him, and can do better, and that there're lots of guys around who would jump at the chance to be my boyfriend, and general cheering-up stuff like that. You're not supposed to rub it in that Fang . . . that Fang . . . Oh, god. I'm going to bed. I can't stand feeling like this.

Em

Subject: re: "Ten Tips to Regaining Your Man"
From: Emmers@britsahoy.co.uk
To: Dru@seattlegrrl.com
Date: 10 August 2004 8:13pm

DatingGuru.com wrote:
> Hello Emmers@britsahoy.co.uk! Your friend
> Dru@seattlegrrl.com has sent you the following
> article from DatingGuru.com: "Ten Steps to Regain-
> ing Your Man" by Dr. Nancy Landers, relationship
> therapist, sex coach, and author of the book The To-
> tally Clueless Girl's Guide to Guy's Minds.
> Ten Steps to Regaining Your Man:
> At some time or other in life, everyone loses the
> friendship of someone they really like. When it's
> your boyfriend who walks away from you, the situa-
> tion can seem desperate. Most women react to such
> a situation by becoming depressed, indulging in cry-
> ing jags, changing their eating and sleeping patterns,
> and shutting themselves off from their friends and
> people who care for them. If that describes you, I
> have two words for you: fight back! Do you think
> your man wants a crybaby who whines about not
> having something? The answer to that is a resound-
> ing no! Men want and respect intelligent, proactive
> women who know what they want, and go after it.

Wow! That was a great article! The Nancy woman who wrote it really knows what she's talking about, huh? OK, that's it, I'm done being Em the hermit nun. Like Nancy said, I'm going to fight back. Fang is mine! Everyone said he was before he went to New Zealand—Devon said he really liked me, and so did Bess, and Holly, and even you said it sounded like he had a thing for me, and dammit! I haven't waited for three whole months for him to come home just to give him up the first time some she-demon grabs him!

I feel so much better now that I've decided to be proactive and intelligent, and go after what I want. I have to say, I was getting tired of crying all the time. I mean, there's just so much walking around with a stuffy nose and red eyes a girl can stand, you know?

You wanted to know what happened at the air-port, so I'll tell you. I can do it now that I've decided to stop whinging (that's what they say here instead of whining). So here's the poop, the full poop, and nothing but the poop.

I cried. A lot. OK, not in front of Fang. Somehow I managed *not* to do that. Holly, who was standing next to me when Audrey grabbed Fang and hauled him up to his feet (I swear to you, Dru, she's built just like your cousin Rolly—the one with no neck and huge shoulders), immediately jumped into friend mode, and grabbed Audrey's arm, steering her away from us while she yadda-yadda'd on about how she

(Audrey) must be excited to be in England. I stood around with my mouth hanging down to my knees in shock.

"Girlfriend?" I whispered to Fang when Holly had Audrey out of immediate earshot. Audrey didn't look happy at being hustled away, but Holly isn't my best friend (next to you, of course) for nothing. I looked back at Fang, still in shock at what had happened. "You . . . you don't . . . I thought . . ."

His jaw worked for a minute like he was stopping himself from saying something, his big puppy-dog eyes filled with sadness and pity. I hate being pitied! "I'm sorry, Emily. This just sort of happened. I didn't go to New Zealand looking for a girlfriend."

A girlfriend. He has a girlfriend. My almost-boyfriend has a girlfriend, and it's not me. My mind was spinning around and around like the grade-school playground merry-go-round we used to play on (aka the Vomit Comet—remember that?). My brain was so dizzy, I felt just like the time when those sixth graders tied us to the VC and spun it so hard that you barfed tomato soup everywhere—only there was no barf at the airport. It was just me and Fang and the pitiful remains of my heart.

"Devon said—" I stopped myself before I could actually say the words. How pathetic is it to tell a guy that another guy said the first guy likes you?

Fang knew what I meant, though. That's the thing with Fang—I didn't have to say things to him. He understood without me even saying it, kind of like a Vulcan mind meld.

"I'm sorry," he said again, his voice hoarse, like he had a cold or something. "I didn't know you were—"

"That's OK," I said, doing the mind-meld thingy again. I was lying through my teeth, of course. It wasn't OK, not even remotely! He knew I'd broken up with Devon while I was in Paris! I had told him! And I told him how much I was looking forward to him coming home from NZ! And he went and got himself a GF anyway.

"Honey? Are you coming? Holly and Emily have come to see us to Windleyspere. Isn't that sweet?"

Audrey had escaped Holly and marched back to Fang, a determined expression on her face.

"Yes, it is sweet," Fang said without looking at me, which was good because I was having trouble swallowing, and had to run to the bathroom so I could cry in a stall. Holly stood outside the door, guarding me in case Audrey came in, but she didn't.

The train ride home was a nightmare. We all sat together, which meant I couldn't cry. Fang wouldn't meet my eye, which was fine with me because I couldn't stand to look at him sitting there being all wonderful and numalicious and *mine mine mine*, and yet *that girl* was there sitting next to him, her leg touching his. It was awful.

Devon sent me a really nice e-mail that said Fang was a fool, and if I wanted him to, he'd come back home and knock some sense into Fang, which was stupid because Fang is his best friend and Devon wouldn't beat him up.

Holly was also being nice, but you know how that is—it just makes you cry more. Anyway, that's all in the past now. This is the new, superimproved Emily. Emily Plus with Bleach. Emily II: The Revenge of a Pissed-off Girlfriend. Emily: TNG! And it's all thanks to you and Dr. Nancy!

I wonder if I can get her book on eBay?

> *Step #1: Do not beat yourself up for the breakup!*
> *Even if it was you who walked away from the*
> *relationship, you have seen the light, and are now*
> *ready to move forward in a positive manner. Begin*
> *this process by meditating ten minutes every day on*
> *all of the good times you and your ex had together.*
> *Reinforce this positive attitude by listing five of his*
> *good qualities and five of yours. Finish by forming a*
> *mental picture of the two of you together again.*

This was a hard step, I'll have you know. I didn't have time to meditate this morning, when I got the article, so I had to do it at work. I sat in the lunchroom because I figured no one would go in there and bother me first thing in the morning.

I sat on the middle of the table in the cow-chewing-its-cud position (do you remember any of the yoga stuff we did two years ago? I don't!), clearing my mind of everything but thoughts of how much fun Fang and I had together.

Memory number one: The time Fang saved me from Aidan at the horrible Halloween party.

There was a scuffing noise that had me peeking out of the corner of my eye.

"What are you doing?" Sam asked, setting down a thermal coffee cup next to me.

"Meditating," I hissed out the side of my mouth, holding on to the mental image of Fang saving me.

"Oh. Have fun."

Memory number two: Fang laughing at my joke about what Scots wore under their kilts (the punchline of which was nothing was worn, it all worked perfectly, ahahahahaha! Get it? Worn? Ha!), his eyes all smiley and happy.

"Oh, good, Emily, you're here early. Doug tells me the beetles are done with the pelican, so can you get started on it right away? Emily?"

"She's meditating," Sam told Helen.

Laughing, happy Fang. Sweet, adorable Fang who was always there for me.

Except now, when I really need— Whoops! Slipped up there for a moment. Back to happy thoughts.

"Is she?" Helen's forehead wrinkled for a minute before her brow cleared. "Meditation is very helpful. My therapist is always after me to take a class in it, but I never seem to have the time. Would you tell her

56

about the pelican? I have to go see why engineering hasn't come up to fix that freezer."

"If you like."

Helen left muttering to herself about taking the next meditation class that had an opening.

Memory number three: Fang taking me to a Chinese restaurant, and laughing so much when I put chopsticks in my ears that he almost choked on his dimsum.

"What's everyone doing in here?" Chris G asked, poking his head around the door for a moment before coming into the room and standing in front of me. "Is this a private party, or can anyone join?"

Then there was the time when we went to a movie and he laughed so hard, the Coke he was drinking frothed when it came out his nose. You just don't get cuter than frothy Coke spewing, do you?

Sam plopped down at the end of the table and waved her hand toward me. "Emily's meditating."

He'd even laughed when I pointed out he'd gotten some of it on his pants, which made him look like he dribbled or something.

"Right now?" Chris leaned forward to look at me. "What's she meditating about?"

"I don't know."

Adorable Fang who . . .

"Do you think it would be all right if I asked her? Or would it disturb her?"

. . . was everything any girl . . .

"I don't know. Why don't you ask her if it would disturb her?"

. . . everything any girl could want . . .

"What's up? Why are you all in here?" Brent and Kia arrived together, Brent immediately snagging a chair and spinning it around to sit backward on it. "Why is Emily on the table? Did she see the ghost?"

. . . any girl could want because he was so perfect . . .

"She's meditating," Sam explained. "We don't know what about, if that was your next question, although CG was thinking of asking her."

. . . perfect and funny and nice and with lovely . . .

"Oh, you shouldn't do that," Kia said as she sat on Brent's lap. "You should never disturb a person when they are meditating. It's very bad for them."

. . . with lovely . . . with lovely . . .

Chris G tipped his head. "I thought that was sleep-walkers you weren't supposed to disturb?"

. . . lovely . . .

"Same difference," Brent said with a shrug.

"No, it's not," Kia said, the only person in the room who was speaking softly so she wouldn't disturb me. "It's very bad for your aura if you're interrupted while meditating."

. . . lovely eyes, that was it, he had lovely . . .

"And Emily has such a pretty orange aura, I'd hate to see it ruined," Kia added.

. . . lovely orange eyes . . . No, wait, that was wrong. Fang had lovely . . .

"I'm lost. Did we agree to ask her or not?"

"Brown puppy dog eyes!" I snarled out loud.

Everyone made shocked faces at me as I grabbed my bag and scooted off the table. "I'm going to the beetle room to get the pelican. OK?"

Sam nodded. Kia looked away. Brent grinned.

I passed Chris L on my way out of the room, Chris G's voice following after me: "She was meditating about a dog's eyes?"

Gotta run. Mom is taking me out to the local pet store so I can buy beetle-larva stuff for the birds. I know, you'd think I could get that at work, but this is special stuff you're supposed to give birds when they're feeding their babies (I won't go into how they do it because I know you've got a hair-trigger gag reflex).

And Dru—thanks for being my friend. I know I was being a great big pain in the butt for a couple of days, and I'm sorry. This whole thing with Fang has made me realize how much my friends mean to me. I can't wait to see you next week!

Hugs and kisses,
~Em

Subject: Enquiry via *Teenwise* health form
From: Emmers@britsahoy.co.uk
To: DrAnnaKnows@teenwise.healthsavvy.co.uk
Date: 11 August 2004 2:13am

Hi, Dr. Anna, it's me again. Thanks a lot for answering my question about whether or not I was going to die. It turns out I'm not, which is cool. I don't think the spots thing had anything to do with contacts, because I don't wear them, but thanks for suggesting that I clean them.

I have another question for you, if you don't mind. This one is about my . . . um . . . someone else. If you know of someone who isn't eating like he normally does, and walks around the house a lot in the middle of the night, and doesn't yell at you for hogging the downstairs bathroom because your sister is using the upstairs one as a darkroom for her spectral photographs, and acts weird in other ways, is that an indication of:

1. cancer
2. insanity
3. alcoholism (although there are no bottles around)
4. some weirdo disease that he picked up working around medieval books and stuff
5. alien spores of any form

Thanks mucho!
Emily Williams

P.S. Yes, there was a boy involved with the spots-before-the-eyes thing, but it's OK; I've stopped being a doormat and am visualizing happy times and stuff while being proactive and intelligent.

Subject: re: Nana freaked big-time!!!!
From: Emmers@britsahoy.co.uk
To: Dru@seattlegrrl.com
Date: 11 August 2004 7:12pm

Dru wrote:
> *she screamed so loud the people at the next table*
> *got up and ran away. The nurse woman had to*
> *come over and give her a shot to calm her down. I*
> *could have died! She started yelling stuff about me*
> *not being a virgin anymore (like I wanted everyone*
> *in the nursing home to know that I still am!!!), and*
> *saying it was all Mom's fault, which is stupid be-*
> *cause Mom doesn't want me to marry Felix either!*

What is it about old people that makes them think it's copacetic to bellow out stuff like that at the top of their lungs? I'm sorry your grandma wigged out so badly, but she didn't disinherit you, did she? She's still going to pay for you to go to college, right?

> Enough of my probs, I'm glad you finally got the
> meditating done so you can move onto step two.
> Um. What was it again?
> > Step #2: Make your ex your priority. If you don't
> > have the time to work on fixing the relationship,
> > you're doomed from the start. Even busy women
> > can find a few minutes to spend working on the
> > relationship—instead of watching a TV show at
> > night, write your ex a poem. Rather than going
> > out to lunch with the girls, call him up and invite
> > him out for hot dogs and people watching. Don't
> > spend your exercise time working out in the gym
> > by yourself—"just happen" to be found jogging
> > along his favorite Rollerblading route.

Ugh. Rollerblading. We all know how that turned out
(and do you know that Holly gets e-mails from Pascal
telling her that Madame, the French teacher in Paris
who tormented us, still has a hissy whenever my name
is mentioned?). But I get the idea. Obviously, the key is
for me to spend some quality time with Fang.

The problem is how to do it.

"You could call him," Holly suggested last night.
Her stepdad is back from Ireland, so she gets to have
time off from taking care of her mom. We were lying
across my bed going over the Dr. Nancy article. "That
would be making him a priority, don't you think?"

"Calling's too easy," I said, sucking the tip of the
pen I was using to doodle on the article (Mr. Emily +

Mrs. Fang = ???). "*Anyone* can call. I bet Audrey calls him all the time. I need something special, something that will show him that he's the most important thing in the world to me."

"Hmm." Holly's face got all serious as she thought about it.

I tapped the pen on my chin, looking out the window as I tried to think of something special I could do for Fang. Something that would mean something to him. Something that would show him how I felt . . . "Oh, no!"

"You thought of something?" Holly asked as I got to my feet and stormed over to the window.

"No. Well, yes, but it's nothing to do with Fang. Look!"

I threw open the window and pointed to the tree outside my curved tower room. Hanging from one of the branches was my very best lace bra and matching undies. You know, the ones I wear only on special occasions. "It's the ghost! That's it; this time it's gone too far! Spreading my underwear around the room is one thing, but when it hangs them in the tree, it's exorcism time! Help me, Hol."

"Maybe you should get a ladder. That doesn't look too safe."

"Are you kidding? If there's a ghost in my underwear drawer, there're demons or something in that hellhole of a basement where the ladder is kept. I'm not going down there for anything."

"You could just leave them. . . ."

I shot her a look that stopped that silly thought. "Not my best lace bra, the one that cost me thirty pounds! No, I'll get it. It won't be too far."

Holly held on to me while I crawled out onto the ledge and leaned down to grab my bra and undies.

"Hang on to me or I'll fall," I yelled as I slipped a couple of inches.

"I've got you," she yelled back, holding on to my belt.

I stretched as far as I could, the slight breeze making the lace fabric flutter against my fingertips. "I . . . urgh . . . almost . . . have . . . them . . . oh. Hi, Brother."

Brother looked up to where I was hanging upside down out of the window above him, Holly clutching my belt, the lacy things held tight in my hands. He opened his mouth like he was going to say something, then shook his head and went in the front door without a word.

"There is definitely something going on with him," I told the now-closed front door. "And in my new role as proactive, intelligent woman, I'm going to find out what. Up, Hol! Bess is home, and it's about time she earned all those birthday and Christmas presents I've given her over the years."

I didn't even bother putting my things away, because ever since Fang came back, the undie ghost has been throwing my stuff around a couple of times a day. Holly and I marched downstairs, past where Mom was kissing Brother (I stopped to shake my finger at him and say, "You're next! Just as soon as I've taken care of the underwear, you're next!"), then into the little glass room in the back Mom calls the conservatory. Bess has taken it over as her personal greenhouse, using it to grow all sorts of plants.

"I want you to conduct an exorcism," I said as I pushed open the door and fought my way through the ferns and other hairy plants she had arranged to grab people when they came into the room. She was sitting on someone—I assumed it was her BF; otherwise I'd really have some blackmail material—snogging him like mad. "Bess! Hello! There are people here! Stop kissing Monk and come upstairs with me and exorcise the ghost in my underwear drawer."

Bess peeled herself off Monk's face with a sound like wet lunch meat on a frying pan, turning so she could frown at us. "I don't believe I heard a knock on the door to this, my personal space. Did you hear a knock, Monk?"

He shook his head.

"I knocked . . . a little," Holly said, trying to stand up for me, which was so sweet that it almost made me cry. Ever since our trip to Paris, she's become Holly the Terminator, really ballsy and all. I'm so proud of her!

"No, you didn't. We didn't knock because we didn't have to, and if you don't come up and get rid of my ghost, I'll tell you-know-who that you bought a BOB."

She gasped, shooting Monk a look. "You wouldn't!"

I just smiled.

"What's a BOB?" he asked.

"Nothing, sweetie, it's just something silly that Emily made a mistake about." She had gotten off his lap while she was speaking, and grabbed my arm (hard!) and dragged me toward the door. "You just sit there and get in the zone, loveykins, and I'll be back in a few minutes. Emily Marie Williams," she hissed as she slammed the door behind her, just barely missing squashing Holly, who slipped behind me with a worried look on her face. "Don't you dare tell Monk about the . . . er . . . device. I told you it was a joke, that's all! It's not like I actually use it. Not often!"

I held up a hand to stop her. "OK, you've crossed over the line into TMI Land."

Holly looked confused.

"Too much information," I explained to her, turning back to Bess. "I don't want to know anything about what you do with your Battery-operated Boyfriend. I just want my underwear drawer depossessed. You're a Wiccan now, so you can do it."

"No, I can't," Bess said, grabbing my arm when I started back toward the conservatory. "Will you stop?

I'm not saying I *won't* help you; I'm saying I *can't*. I'm not a full Wiccan yet."

I glared. "Will someone tell me what is the good in having a sister who is a witch if she can't get rid of perverted underwear ghosts?"

Bess smacked my arm and went to sit on the bottom step of the stairs, twisting her hair like she does when she's thinking. "Hmm. Ghosts. Hmm . . . I know!"

I looked at my watch. "Ten seconds. That's, like, a record for you."

She narrowed her eyes at me. "Do you want me to help you or not?"

I sighed. Sisters! "Yes."

She pursed her lips as she looked me up and down. "What's the magic word?"

"Sex toy?" I asked, grinning. I had her and she knew it. Ah, victory was sweet!

"Mr. Wayne."

I looked at Holly. She looked back at me. We both looked at Bess. "Huh?"

"Mr. Wayne," Bess said slowly in that annoying way older sisters have. "He's a new psychic in town. Aurora told me about him. He's Wiccan-friendly, and comes with a very high recommendation from the Council of White Witches and Fae Folk. You go see him and tell him about your ghost, and he'll take care of it for you."

"Oh. OK. You're sure he's not, like, some weirdo or something?"

Bess shrugged. "Aurora seemed to think he was good, but I don't know much about him. The way I see it, he can't do any harm."

"Yeah, that's what you said about Aurora, and she ended up setting fire to my underwear just before I left for Paris."

"That was four months ago," Bess said, waving her hand. "She's improved a lot since then."

"OK, but if this Mr. Wayne—and is it just me, or does it sound like he should be on *Queer Eye*?—sets fire to anything, I'm going to curse you."

"You're not a Wiccan, Em. You can't curse anyone."

I gave her a look of utter scorn. "If my underwear is burned up again, just watch me!"

Oops, gotta run. Brother just came home (late! I wonder if he's having an affair? Would having an affair make you not hungry and not grouchy like normal? Hmm. Must think on this.) and I want to have a word in his ear. That's another British thing. People here are forever having words in other people's ears. I think it sounds kinda kinky, but whatever.

I'll let you know how it goes with Mr. Wayne. Holly and I have an appointment to see him tomorrow.

Hugs and kisses,
~Em

Subject: re: Better now?
From: Emmers@britsahoy.co.uk
To: Devonator@skynetcomm.com
Date: 12 August 2004 9:47pm

Devonator wrote:
> although I'd like to know, if you don't mind telling
> me, what it is you decided to do. I'm glad you're
> feeling better, but now I'm wondering if I shouldn't
> be warning Fang that he's about to be struck with
> the vengeance of a woman scorned, as my mum al-
> ways puts it.

It's nothing bad, so don't worry! Dru sent me a really cool article about how to get your man back after he's left you, and it has all these great steps that you do in order to make your guy realize what a stupid, idiotic, faithless, total and complete poop he has been, and to bring him to his knees.

I particularly like the knees part.

Anyway, I'm doing that, working at the museum—tomorrow they're having a party, which should be fun—and dealing with my underwear ghost. Did I tell you that Holly and I went to see a real psychic today after work? OMG! His name is Mr. Wayne Dekstetter, and honest to Pete, Devon, he's like Mr. Woo-Woo Weirdo. He doesn't look bad or anything. In fact, he reminds me a lot of Mr. Butler, the junior janitor at school—you remember him from the Halloween party? He was the smiley, short, balding guy with thick glasses who slid on the water from the fire sprinklers and ended up in the hospital with a wrenched spleen or something (Miss Horseface repeatedly mentioned that I had permanently damaged a man's spleen until the very last day of school)—anyway, this psychic guy looks just like Mr. Butler. Very happy, very jolly—like Santa but without the beard. The kind of guy who looks like a priest but is probably into dressing dogs up like little girls. Perv-city.

"It sounds like your entity has a weakness in his chakras," Mr. Wayne said after I finished explaining to him what was happening with the undie ghost.

"It has a weakness in its what-ras?" I asked, wondering if Mr. Wayne was actually *from* the planet Earth, or if he was just visiting for a bit.

"Chakras. Oh, dear, I see I must explain myself. In addition to being a noted psychic and spectral investigator, I'm a trained chakra healer. I've found through extensive work with troubled entities that the majority are bound to the physical plane due to chakra impurities and imbalances. Generally it's the fourth through sixth chakras that are troubled in spirits, although I did once have a nasty run-in with a poltergiest who was completely missing its second chakra."

"Um," I said, which, really was about all you *could* say in such a situation.

"What's a chakra?" Holly asked. "It's nothing dangerous, is it?"

"Oh, it can be deadly," Mr. Wayne said with a cheery smile. "If they get blocked, they can completely stop your flow of energy. Chakras are energy centers, points where the chi, or life energy, flows."

"Like an EMF?" I asked.

"Erm . . ."

"Electromagnetic field," I explained. "I'm going to be a physicist."

"Oh. Er . . . something like that, yes. In humans the energy field acts as a connection between the spirit realm and the physical world. It expresses the manner in which our higher selves will exist in the other realm."

"What other realm? Scotland?"

His smile got a little tight. "No, the *other realm*. The higher plane of existence that we all go to when we leave our frail physical containers behind."

"Oh, that other realm. Um. OK."

"You said that the energy flows through us, but how can Emily's ghost still have it, since it's dead?" Holly asked very seriously.

"A good and fair question, young lady. As I said, dsyfunctional chakras indicate an individual's energy flow has become blocked and unbalanced, which has the result of preventing a viable connection with the spiritual plane."

"So you're saying that if my chakras are out of alignment and I die, I'll become a ghost because I

71

won't have the energy to move into the other realm?" I asked.

"Exactly!" Mr. Wayne beamed at us for a second. "Chakras out of balance prevent an entity from acheiving its higher potential, thus leaving it bound to the physical plane. It is my job to heal the chakras so the entity can move on."

"Coolio! Um. It's not going to, like, hurt the ghost or anything? 'Cause although my ghost is annoying, I don't want it to be tormented."

Mr. Wayne tried hard to look sad. "I'm afraid your entity is already tormented, Miss Williams. More often than not the cause of chakras being unbalanced is a traumatic experience in the individual's past that serves to tear the psyche, allowing impure energies to take the place of healthy ones, which results in unbalanced and blocked energy patterns."

"Oh, the poor ghost," Holly said as she clutched my arm. "Em, you have to make sure its chakras are cleaned up."

"Yeah, I don't like the thought of it touching my undies with impure spectral hands." I gnawed on my lip, worrying about what would happen to the ghost if I didn't do it. The amount of money Mr. Wayne wanted (twenty-five pounds!) would take a major chunk out of my "shopping with Dru" money, but I didn't want my ghost to go around suffering anymore. Obviously something was up for it to be flinging my things around twice a day now. It was like a cry for help, don't you think? The professor's family that Brother had swapped homes with would be coming back in a few weeks, and I just knew that the girl who had my room wouldn't take care of the ghost. So it was up to me.

Mr. Wayne, being a psychic and all, evidently sensed my indecision, because he stood up from the big desk he had been sitting behind and came around to where Holly and I were sitting. "There are seven main chakras in the human body. Each chakra corresponds to an aspect of our makeup, and they all lie along the central energy channel, known to most laypeople as the spinal cord, up to the head. If you would lie down on this table, I would be happy to read your chakras as a demonstration of my abilities." He waved his hand across the room toward a wall where a thin metal table covered with a blue pad stood.

"Oh, Emily, yes! Let Mr. Wayne read your chakras. I'm ever so keen to see a reading."

I'm not quite sure why, but I felt vaguely alarmed. I mean, did I want a stranger reading my chakras? What if he saw bad things about me? He was kind of pervy in a jolly sort of way, Devon, like he got off on looking at girls' chakras. I really didn't want him touching me. "Why don't you let him read you?"

Her eyes opened wide. You know, when I first met Holly, she would have gasped that she couldn't, but she's really changed a lot in the last year, hasn't she?

Instead of wimping out, she swallowed hard and said (in a voice that didn't shake at all, despite the fact that her hands were clutching each other), "If you like."

I looked back at Mr. Wayne. His eyes were still happy, but they had an odd light in them, like he wanted to be rubbing his hands together, but knew he'd scare us off if he did. "Um. What exactly do you do when you read chakras? You don't . . . er . . . touch the person you're reading?"

"No, certainly not! I simply glide my hands above the individual's body, and feel his or her life force."

A little shiver ran down my back at the thought of him fondling my life force, but I could see that despite Holly's bravado (aren't you impressed with her? I am!) she really didn't want him groping her energy, so I gave in and said he could read me.

It wasn't as bad as I thought it was going to be. Mr. Wayne put on some crappy New Age music (it wasn't Enya, which sucked), and did a little chanting thing while I stretched out on the table, waving his hands in the air and swaying. After he was done with that, he started passing his hands about four inches above my body.

"This is your seventh chakra," he said, waving his hands over the top of my head. "It characterizes spiritual perfection, and its color is violet."

"Oooh, your chakras have colors," Holly said,

standing at the foot of the table. I had whispered to her to keep an eye on Mr. Wayne in case he got any funny ideas (you never know with old guys who always look happy).

"Your seventh chakra is very strong, very pure. Now I will move to the sixth." He waved his hands over my forehead. "This is your third eye."

"Hey! I do not have pimples! I use an oatmeal-and-apricot scrub every day!" I said indignantly. Third eye, ha! Double ha with antlers on it!

"Eh? No, your third eye is your seat of insight," he said, giving me an odd look. "Its color is indigo. Your sixth chakra is also very strong. You must have psychic abilities."

"Well, I did know that Holly was going to call me this afternoon right before she did. I didn't know I was psychic, though. Coolio!"

"Precognition is a very common form of psychic abilities," Mr. Wayne said as he started waving his hands over my throat. "This is your fifth chakra, and it characterizes your ability to communicate. It is *very* strong."

I frowned at the emphasis he put on the word *very*. Was he saying I talked too much?

"The color of the fifth chakra is blue."

"Blue, indigo, violet . . . hey! You're doing Roy G. Biv in reverse!"

"Roy G. Biv?" Holly asked.

"It's a mnemonic for the color spectrum: red, orange, yellow, green, blue, indigo, violet. Roy G. Biv, get it?"

"Shall we proceed?" Mr. Wayne asked, then moved so he could pass his hands over the air above my boobs. I made squinty eyes at him to make sure he didn't slip in a boob fondle while I wasn't watching. "Your fourth chakra is your heart, your affections. Here I find that your chakra is a little weak. Nothing serious, but it is not as strong and pure as the other chakras. It could indicate that you're having troubles of a romantic nature."

I sighed. "You can say that again."

He went on down through the rest of the chakras (chakra three: sense of self, yellow, strong; chakra two: sexual energy, orange, a bit on the impure side—which I took offense to. I mean sheesh! How could I be impure when I haven't done it?; chakra one: physical well-being, red, also strong), then told me I need to work on opening up my heart and embracing my enemies, yadda yadda yadda. He said he could adjust the whacked-out chakras for me, but that would be an additional thirty pounds, so I said no.

Anyhoo, he's coming over tomorrow night to take a general reading of the ghost. Cool, huh?

Gotta run. I have the party tomorrow at work, and I haven't even picked out what I am going to wear.

I'm thinking of my red ruched silk tank top and black Wet Seal pants with the chain belt. Does that say day party to you?

Miss you like mad!
Emily

Subject: Yesterday was one of *those* days
From: Emmers@britsahoy.co.uk
To: Dru@seattlegrrl.com
Date: 14 August 2004 8:38pm

Remember step two—making Fang my priority? Well, I did what Dr. Nancy suggested—I called Fang up and invited him to have lunch with me at the museum. I was so nervous about doing it I was almost sick to my stomach, and I stopped dialing his number about fifteen times before I finally remembered that I was an intelligent, proactive woman who fought back. So I called him.

She answered. You know. *Her.* The BF stealer.

"Um. Hi, this is Emily. Is Fang there?" I asked, grinding my teeth, which I swear to you I've never done before, but there was just something about Audrey that made me grind, grind, grind.

"Yes, he is," she said, and waited.

I ground a little more. "Could I, like, *talk* to him?"

"I'll see if he's available," she said. Gah! Like, what

was he doing if she was there? Of course he was available.

"Hello, Emily," Fang said a few seconds later, and my heart did a little somersault in my chest. If that wasn't a sign that my fourth chakra is wonky, I don't know what is! "How are you?"

"Fine. Listen, the guys at work are having this party tomorrow around lunchtime, and I thought maybe you would like to come along and see where I work, and we can do the party and maybe lunch in the café afterward."

"Tomorrow?" There was a pause while I heard whispering going on. Female whispering. "Sorry, Emily, but I promised to show Audrey around tomorrow morning. Tourist things."

My stomach wadded up on itself. I hated this! Fang, the old Fang, would have said yes. He would have been interested to see where I worked. He would have loved to come to the work party, and do lunch after. But she had ruined everything!

I took a few deep breaths and remembered that proactive, intelligent women do not cry because an evil New Zealand witch has her clutches on the love of her life. No, those women do something. I stopped grinding my teeth, and said in as cheerful a voice as I could manage, "Great! I work in a museum—it's very touristy! Audrey will love it! Come by around eleven, see the museum; then let the guard know you're here to see me, and I'll show you guys around the back part of the museum. It's very cool. And we can do lunch, OK?"

"All three of us?" he asked, his wonderful, sweet, adorable voice hesitant.

"Sure! I'm looking forward to getting to know Audrey." It almost killed me to say that, but I did, and boy, if that doesn't rate major karma points, I don't know what will.

"I don't know. Let me check—" he started to say.

Desperate, I played my last card. "I miss talking to you, Fang. You're my best guy friend! I didn't think that just because Audrey is here, we would have to stop being friends."

"Of course we don't," he said in a lot firmer voice. "Nothing will change our friendship, Emily."

"Good. Then I'll see you both tomorrow! Later!" I hung up before he could say anything else, which I guess worked because today right on the dot of eleven, Paris the guard (nice guy, but he has only one leg) called and said I had friends waiting. I put the remainder of the parrot skeleton I was cleaning back in its big glass jar of water, took off the face mask and apron that I wore so I wouldn't get bird juice on me, and toddled out to meet them.

"Welcome to the Bolte," I said, as I slipped through the door leading to the public part of the museum. I had been wondering if a proactive, intelligent woman would kiss her BF-to-be upon greeting him, or if she would just say hi, but the sight of Audrey standing close to Fang made up my mind. I stood on my tippy-toes and kissed Fang's cheek (he got big eyes at that), then held out my hand for Audrey to shake. Yeah, yeah, it was very big of me, but you know, Dru, the older I get the more I realize that sometimes you have to think about other people's feelings. Mom had told me that I shouldn't damn Audrey without getting to know her, and that maybe she was really a nice person.

I wasn't willing to buy that, but I decided that just because I was intelligent and proactive and was fighting for my man, it didn't mean I had to be a b*tch (word bleeped for your comfort). I was willing to give her a chance. I suppose it wasn't her fault she had fallen for my Fang, and I know that if I were her, and another much cooler and more proactive girl came along and took my BF from me, I'd be hurt.

Oh. Wait. I guess . . . um . . . never mind. Moving on.

I showed them around the main part of the museum, then took them back to the beetle room and cleaning room. Fang was really interested in stuff, but Audrey wrinkled up her nose at the smell in the cleaning room (couldn't blame her for that; it really did stink in there). By the time we were done, it was eleven-thirty and party time!

"The party is being held in the lunchroom area," I explained to them as we walked past the cases of shelves toward the big room with the two large tables. "Although no one really eats lunch in there, so I don't know why I call it that. But it should be fun, because everyone will be there. Oh, that's the little office where I number the bird bones. See that desk by the window with the big light on the table? That's mine. Anyway, as I was saying, everyone will be at the party, although it's kind of a weird time of day to have one, don't you think? Here we are! Just around this corner is the lunchro— Omigod! *Oh my God!*"

The scene in the lunchroom—which I now realize no one else called a lunchroom for a very good reason— was like something out of my worst nightmare. Everyone was there—Helen, both Chrises, Kia and Brent, Sam, and a couple of people from the mammal section whom I didn't talk to much. The radio was blasting dance music, and everyone was laughing and joking and chatting . . . while on the tables before them were the remains of several dead birds and animals.

Audrey made a choking sound and spun around with her hand over her mouth, racing back to the offices (where there was a bathroom). Fang looked at the horror scene with bright eyes, walking over to where Kia was pulling the bone from a big, furry gray thing. (Badger? Wolf? Really big hedgehog?) Or rather, a formerly big furry gray thing. The skin had been peeled off and was lying next to it. What remained was all red and ooky and . . . well, I won't go on or you'll be ralphing all over your monitor.

"Is that a badger?" Fang asked, touching the furry bit.

"Yes. Someone donated it to us. Roadkill." Kia looked at Fang curiously as he lifted the badger pelt.

"This is my friend Fang," I said, standing at the end of the table, my hands on my hips. "And just what the hell is going on here? I thought we were having a party!"

"We are," Chris G said.

"This is a party?" I asked, waving my hands at the two tables. Honest to Pete, Dru, it looked like some sort of deranged animal-only version of *Frankenstein*! There were bits and pieces of birds and various animals lying all over the place. Everyone was red up to the elbows with blood. And the smell! I won't go into that, but you can take it from me that it was enough to drop a horse. Ew. Horse. Thank God there wasn't one of those there.

"It is a party. It's a skinning and skelling party."

"What?" I shrieked, feeling like pulling out my hair. Were these people all insane?

"It's a skinning and skeleton party, Emily." Chris L looked at everyone else around the table, who had their eyebrows raised. Brent was snickering, but at least the others didn't laugh at me.

"We hold skinning and skelling parties once a month. I thought you knew that?" Helen asked. "These parties are how we prepare the specimens."

"We saved you a woodpecker," Brent said, plucking a dead bird from a small pile in front of Helen.

I debated a) barfing, b) fainting, or c) dying, but decided I couldn't barf with Fang there (Devon was the only one whom I could comfortably barf in front of), and if I fainted, I'd probably fall into the bloody gross stuff all over the table, so that was out, and death would mean Audrey would get to keep Fang, so that was crossed off the list as well. Instead I said, with much dignity and coolness, "No. I didn't know. No one told me. You just said it was a party."

Brent shot an amused glance to Chris G, whom I formally struck off my list of nummy guys. "Oh, we didn't tell you? How very remiss of us."

Fang held up the badger skin. "Fascinating. What are you doing with the rest of it?"

Kia held up something so ooky, I can't describe it. "Removing as much of the soft tissue as I can; then the skeleton will go in to the beetles. Are you a zoology student?"

"Vet," he answered, moving over to see what Sam was doing. She had something small. (A vole? I don't know; I refused to look at that point.)

"*Remiss* isn't quite the word I would use," I said, still being dignified and all. I refused to show them that I had a major case of the creeps being in the same room as all those dead, peeled animals. The only good thing was that Audrey was in the bathroom ralphing up her guts, while Fang was going around seeing what everyone was doing, obviously fascinated by it all. So I stood well clear of the goopy table and let him look at everything, and when he was through, I told Helen I was taking an early lunch, and dragged Fang out of there to go find Audrey.

"This is an amazing place," Fang said as we walked toward the offices. There was no sign of Audrey, so I assumed she was still in the bathroom. "I had no idea that was how the skins were prepared. Utterly fascinating."

"Yeah. Fascinating." I stopped in front of the door to the staff bathroom, gnawing on my lip. I had hoped to have time to talk to Fang privately, to let him know how much I liked him and all, but the whole party thing had kind of shaken me. "Fang—"

"Emily—" he said at the exact same time, then stopped.

"You go first," I said, more than a little nervous now that we were there, just the two of us, and he was looking at me and everything.

"No, you spoke first. You go ahead."

You know how I said Fang's eyes were puppy-dog brown? They weren't just brown. They were shades of brown, at least a hundred of them, with little black spikes that came out from their pupils. They were the most beautiful eyes I'd ever seen. "I . . . uh . . . no, you go. Mine can wait."

He took my hand, rubbing his thumb over my knuckles, making my legs go weak. There also didn't seem to be enough air in the room. "Devon called me from Greece. He said . . . he said you'd been waiting for me to come home."

"Yeah," I said, trying to get some air into my lungs. How come a guy holding your hand can make all the air go away? Does Felix do that to you? "I told you that. I told you how much I was looking forward to your coming home."

"I didn't know you meant it . . . that way," he said, his big, lovely eyes filled with sadness. "If I had, I would have come back in July. But I thought you were happy. Your e-mails always seemed so happy."

Tears pricked at the back of my eyes. I bit my lip so I wouldn't cry, because intelligent, proactive women don't cry. "I was happy. But I missed you. I said that, too." My lower lip tried to quiver as a tear broke free despite my trying to blink them away. It rolled down my cheek.

"You did. I just didn't know that you meant it," he said, brushing away the tear with his thumb. "Aw, Emily, don't cry."

"I'm not; it's just an . . . an . . . aberration," I said, quickly wiping up a couple more tears that were snaking down my cheeks. I had a lot of things to say to Fang, and I didn't want to miss saying them because I was crying. "Why . . . why . . ." I gestured toward the bathroom door.

He let go of my hand and put both of his in his pockets. "Do you remember when you first came to England, you went to one of Devon's parties?"

I gave a short, bitter laugh. How could I forget that party? "The one where I got drunk and passed out, and you brought me home."

He nodded, his eyes dark with pain. "Your parents reamed me a new hole that night for letting you get drunk."

"I'm sorry. I didn't know. You never said anything."

"I never said anything because I deserved it. I realized after I went home that the reason I had let you get so drunk that night was because I had been trying to avoid you."

"Avoid me?" Pain, sharp and bright, pierced my heart, and I swallowed back more tears. He had been trying to avoid me? "Why?"

"Because I was in love with you, and you were mad about Aidan."

"Oh, God," I said on a sob. "I was such an idiot! I didn't know!"

"I know you didn't. But you got over him, and I thought I had a chance. You just needed to have some time to find your feet, and then . . . well, then Devon stepped in."

The tears were back, streaming nonstop down my face. I mashed my lips together to keep from sobbing out loud. "I was an idiot about Devon, too," I finally managed to say. "He's a friend, a very dear friend, and I just got that confused in my mind."

He nodded again. "I know."

"But I broke up with Devon! I told you all about that!"

"You told me a week before I was due to leave for New Zealand. I didn't have a chance to see you before I left, and you sounded so happy, so damned happy. . . ." His voice trailed off. His Adam's apple bobbed up and down like he was swallowing something big. "I didn't know you wanted to be more than just friends. You never said."

"Well, of course I didn't say that in e-mail! You don't e-mail someone and tell them you want to be their girlfriend!"

"I'm sorry," he said, and I believed it. He was sorry, but that didn't fix the situation.

"So you went and found Audrey." I wiped my face again, wishing I had a Kleenex so I could blow my nose.

"Audrey . . ." He made a sorrowful shrugging gesture. "I was lonely, Emily. I'm just a man."

"Yeah," I said, making a decision. "You are."

The door to the bathroom opened before I could say the rest of what I wanted to say. I spun around so Audrey wouldn't see I'd been crying, and yelled something about being right back before running up the stairs to the bathroom up there.

Before you ask, no, my decision wasn't to give up trying to win him back. OK, it was at first, when he said he was lonely. But that lasted for only a couple of seconds before I realized that what he was trying to say, but couldn't because it would be cruel to Audrey—and Fang is never cruel—was that he still loved me. And you know I go all squishy inside when I think about him. Oh, OK, I'll say it. I love him. I love Fang. *A lot!* So we should be together . . . even if I am leaving for home at the end of the month. And that meant that I had to change my plan and make Audrey realize that Fang wasn't for her. Then Fang would be mine, Audrey wouldn't be hurt, and I could turn my attention to figuring out a way to take Fang home with me.

The rest of the lunch was whatchamacallit . . . anticlimactic. Audrey was still a bit green and didn't seem too happy about the idea of eating, Fang was quiet and watched me a lot, and I tried to get Audrey talking about herself so I could figure out how I was going to prove that Fang wasn't right for her.

"So, Fang, you really liked the skinning party, huh?"

He gave me a wary look over a spoon of soup, glancing at Audrey before speaking. "It was interesting."

"Yeah, I thought you'd like that stuff. Animals and their insides and stuff. Vets," I said, turning to Audrey, who had gone pale, "do a lot of stuff with animals' innards. Guts and things. Lots of surgery. Isn't that right, Fang?"

"A fair amount of vet work is surgery, yes," he said, his eyes asking me what I was doing.

I smiled back at him before turning my smile (third

best, no sense in wasting a good smile) on Audrey. "Yes, sirree, lots and lots of animal guts and stuff. Innards everywhere, I bet. Fang told me this hysterical story about what he and some of the other vet students did with a dead sheep. It seems one of the professors was Scottish, so they made up their own version of haggis by taking the sheep and slicing it open on the prof's desk—"

"I'm sure Audrey doesn't want to hear about that," Fang said, sending me a look with all sorts of warnings in it.

"Oh, sorry, how thoughtless of me. Of course, Audrey doesn't like hearing about all the many things you and your vet student friends do with the animal guts and entrails and blood and all those slimy parts that look like bits of a chicken that's been left out on a hot road for a couple of days—"

"Emily!"

"Mmm? Oh. Sorry. So!" I gave Audrey another smile. "Has Fang told you about his dearest non-vet friend Devon? Devon doesn't like animal guts either. He's very rich, too. He's in Greece now, on vacation. He takes lots of trips to all sorts of places. And man, is he cute! Gorgeous, really. And he's Fang's best friend, which is odd, really, because Devon doesn't like cutting up animals, or playing around in their insides, or doing any of the icky surgery stuff that Fang does—"

"We have to go now," Fang said quickly, looking at his watch as he stood up. Audrey jumped up like she couldn't wait to get out of there. "Thank you for the tour, Emily. And . . . er . . . for the rest."

"No problem," I said, following them out of the café to the bright sunshine outside. "Audrey, you have to meet Devon when he comes back from his vacation in Greece. You'll just love him. Did I tell you he was staying in a villa? A private villa with its own swimming pool and sauna? It's actually one of his uncle's villas—his rich uncle, who adores Devon and lets him stay at all of his houses—and Devon says it's sheer heaven, what with the servants and nothing to do but lie around and get tan and swim, and go into the casinos at night. Yep. Devon sure is a wonderful guy."

Audrey headed for the banged-up Mini that Fang shared with one of his vet buddies. Fang stopped and looked at me curiously. "Devon?" was all he asked.

"She's not right for you," I said evenly, not a tear in sight. I was back to being Wonder Emily, proactive, intelligent, and not standing for anything getting in the way of her and her hunk of burnin' love. "The sooner she finds that out, the happier she'll be. I'm not asking you to dump her—that would be mean, and I know you wouldn't do that because you're a nice guy and all. So if you can't tell her to take a hike, then I'm just going to have to find someone else for her, someone who will make her happier, so she'll leave you, and then we can be together without feeling guilty. It's a good plan, huh?"

"Emily—"

"I love you, Fang. And I'm not giving up on you."

"Oh, God," he said, his eyes closing for a minute. When they opened again, they were shadowed with pain. "Do you know what you're doing to me?"

I didn't, not really, not until that moment when I looked into his warm eyes and saw all the regret and anguish and guilt and love there. Then I realized just what he was feeling, how awful he felt, and what a horrible situation he was caught in. I was pulling on him from one side, and Audrey was on the other. "No. I thought I did, but I guess I didn't. Are we stuck, Fang?"

He grabbed my hand, his warm palm pressed gently against mine. "I don't know."

I squeezed his fingers and breathed in the wonderful Fang smell I had just noticed. It was almost indescribable—kind of lemony, kind of woodsy—it was just Fang. "Do you want me to be proactive and fight for you? If you don't"—I had to stop and swallow the lump that was making my throat ache—"if you don't, I won't."

He said nothing for a few seconds, just looked at me with those hurting eyes, and I wanted to cry. He was going to make me give up. He was going to choose her over me. He wasn't going to be my Fang any longer.

Audrey leaned her head out the car window. "Fang? Are you coming?"

"Yes," he said, leaning forward to brush his lips lightly over my cheek. It wasn't a real kiss; it was more a promise of a kiss, a promise of . . . oh, I don't know. Something. Something big. "Yes, I want you to fight for me. Fight for us, Emily. Fight hard and don't give up."

He walked away then, just walked away and got into the car without looking back at me, but I didn't care. I had a new mission.

Boy, that Dr. Nancy sure knows her stuff! Two steps and Fang was mine!

Kissies!
~Em

Subject: re: We're leaving tomorrow!
From: Emmers@britsahoy.co.uk
To: Dru@seattlegrrl.com
Date: 14 August 2004 9:09pm

Dru wrote:
> *so we have to be at the airport two hours early,*
> *which totally sucks. I mean, who wants to spend*
> *two hours sitting around watching people wait for*
> *an airplane? Anyway, our flight leaves at six, and we*
> *get dinner on the plane, then when we land in*
> *London, it'll be tomorrow afternoon! How trick is*
> *that?*

How trick? Dru, we really have to have a little chat about your using slang. It's so totally yesterday!

I can't wait to see you! I can't wait for you to meet Holly and Fang and all my friends here, and see my underwear get thrown around the room and everything. I wish Devon were going to be back from Greece in time so you could meet him (even if you are engaged, you'll drool over him), but he's working on his all-over tan (hee!) and won't be back for another week or so. I don't suppose your mom has changed her mind and you guys are going to stay in England longer? Or maybe she'll let you stay with us while she sees Wales. (I don't care if her grandmother was Welsh, everyone I know says you can't understand anything there, so why bother going?)

> You'll have to help me pick out a really good
> present for Felix. Something an English guy would
> like. Maybe some of those English flag underwear?

It's called a Union Jack, and I don't know any Brits who wear them. In fact, I don't know anyone who wears them. And Felix isn't British at all, so why would he like what a Brit would like? Anyhoo, you know I'll help you find something. Brother said if your mom says it's OK, we can take the train to Manchester and hit the mall there. Coolio, huh?

> can't believe you told Fang you loved him! Right
> there in the open! I can't believe he said it to you,

93

> *either! I can't believe that witch Audrey doesn't*
> *realize that she's lost, and leave him so you guys*
> *can be happy together. So, dish. What are you going*
> *to do to pry her loose from him?*

The "Get Rid of Audrey So Fang and I Can Live Happily Ever After until I Have to Go Home, at Which Point I'm Going to Have to Figure Out a Way for Him to Come to Seattle, Too" plan began today with stage one: become Audrey's new best friend.

"Hi!" I said exactly twelve hours ago. "I'm Emily Williams. This is Holly Lester. We're friends of Audrey's. Is she in?"

"Oh, how nice, friends of Audrey's," the old lady who answered the door to the apartment over the Laundromat in Windleyspere—that's about a twenty-minute drive from Piddlington-on-the-Weld. "Come in, do. Audrey, dear! Friends!"

Audrey, needless to say, did not look thrilled to see us. OK, she didn't mind Holly; it was me she wasn't thrilled to see. I'm big enough that I can admit that. Do you see emotional growth here? Mom said last night that she thinks I'm maturing wonderfully, which was kind of nice, but kind of stupid, because come on—I'm seventeen! I've already matured all I'm going to! But you know the Old Ones; they're forever going on about living up to your responsibilities and not acting like the sun revolves around you and all that crap. Where was I? Oh, yeah, Audrey.

"Hello, Emily," she said, all suspicious-like. "How . . . nice . . . to see you again."

"Yeah, I thought you'd be lonely, since Fang has to go take his pre-year exams today, so Hol and I—you remember Holly, right? She's very cool. She doesn't like animal guts either, although she is dating a Scottish shepherd with six fingers on one hand—anyhoodles, Holly and I thought we'd take you under our wings, so to speak."

Holly did a cute little chicken-wing arm-flapping thing. "Wings!"

"Oh," Audrey said. "How thoughtful of you. I had planned to spend the day reading—"

"Now, I like a book as well as the next person," I said, smiling brightly so she wouldn't think Holly and I were two weirdo Kiwi kidnappers (Kiwi is what they call people from New Zealand. Don't ask why, 'cause I don't know and, frankly, don't care, because really, you're calling someone a green fruit, and you just *know* that the person who first thought it up was doing it to be nasty to someone). "Is this your purse? Great! Let's go!"

"Go where?" Audrey said kind of feebly as Holly and I bustled her out of the tiny sitting room and down a dark hall to the front door. Audrey's aunt popped out from another room.

"We're going to Never Never Land! It's the day camp Holly works at. Underprivileged kids and all that. Loads of fun, and it's good for you. We're gearing up for a huge battle, when the camp closes for the summer. They were going to do the Battle of Hastings, 1066, but Holly and I convinced them to reenact the battle at Helm's Deep."

"Complete with water balloons," Holly said. "And one of the counselors is going to be Legolas."

"Battle?" Audrey said as Holly opened the door. I shoved Audrey through it, waving at the aunt as I followed. "Helm's Deep?"

"Have fun, dear!" her aunt called after us.

"Why are you doing this?" Audrey asked ten minutes later as we plopped down on the train that would take us back to Piddlington.

Holly peered at me out of the corner of her eye before answering. "We just want to get to know you."

I leaned forward and threw every single atom of sincerity (real or manufactured, we're not going to get picky here) I could muster into my face. "Any friend of Fang's is a friend of ours."

She didn't look like she bought that at all, and to be honest, I couldn't blame her. I mean, if two almost-strangers dragged me off with them to a kids' day camp, and then told me I was their new best friend, I'd probably be a little suspicious, too.

Holly, however, soon put Audrey at ease, and by the time we arrived at POTW, they were chatting away like long-lost friends. We spent the day working with the other volunteers and the kids to build the deeping wall and big keep part of Helm's Deep out of cardboard and wood. You know me—I'm not an overly crafty sort of person, but I have to admit it was fun building the castle.

Just after the lunch break, Audrey came up to me as I was tying a kiddie slide to some cardboard so the guy playing Legolas could slide down it while shooting his arrows just like Orli did in *The Two Towers* (which was, of course, the coolest move in the whole movie).

"Emily, I want to apologize," she said, squatting down next to where I was propping the bottom of the slide up with a block of wood.

"Why?" I asked, wondering if she, you know, tooted or something and I didn't notice it.

"Because I treated you horribly this morning. I was sure you dragged me off here for some ulterior purpose, as some sort of a plan to keep Fang and me apart, and I see I was wrong."

"Um," I said, not being able to look at her in case she saw the guilt written all over my face. I felt like I had a great big bright red neon sign overhead with an arrow pointing down to me with the words TRYING TO TAKE YOUR BOYFRIEND.

"I know now that you are really as generous as Fang said you were."

That so surprised me, I did look at her. "What?"

She smiled and handed me a hammer that I needed to nail the cardboard into the wood. "Fang sings your praises, but you must know that. He said you were the friendliest, warmest person he's ever known, generous with your time and affection."

Oh, God! He thought that? About me? And she believed him? Oh, God, oh, God, oh, God!

"I just wanted you to know that I appreciate your making me feel welcome when . . . well, I know there was something between you and Fang at one time."

I just stared at her, my mouth hanging open because I was too stunned to close it, and you know I hate that openmouthed look because honestly, do you want to see someone's shiny wet tongue and stuff when you're talking to them? Blech.

"Thank you for your friendship," she said, giving my hand a little squeeze before she got to her feet and trotted off to help Holly with the Hornburg.

Well, you can imagine how that made me feel. There I was planning on prying her off of Fang so I could have him, without a thought about how she's going to feel about it, and she's thanking me for being nice to her. I felt so bad that . . . Oh, shoot, look at the time! I have to send this now or you won't get it before you leave.

I'm so excited! Two more days and you'll be here! Yay!

Hugsies and big wet kisses (hoot!),
~Em

Subject: re: Do I have a girl for you!
From: Emmers@britsahoy.co.uk
To: Devonator@skynetcomm.com
Date: 15 August 2004 7:26pm

Devonator wrote:
> *you to think of me, but I'm not really girlfriend*
> *shopping right now. Who is this bird you're*
> *trying to stick me with?*

I'm not trying to stick you with her, Devon; I'm trying to matchmake! Honest, she's very nice, smart . . . *ish* (although she doesn't have the best insights into people, but then, neither do I and you liked me as a GF), pretty, and is only two years older than you. You said you liked older women, remember? And she's from New Zealand. When you come back next week, I'll introduce her to you. She's . . . um . . . kind of Fang's GF now, but they really aren't happy together. Or Fang isn't. But you know him; he's too nice to say that he took up with Audrey while he was waiting for me to stop being an idiot, and now he doesn't know how to get rid of her.

I thought about just having him tell her the truth, because that way I wouldn't have to go around feeling guilty all the time (that's *wearing!*), but then I decided that wouldn't be fair to Fang. . . . Sec, Brother's bothering me about something.

Back! Just when I think I have figured out old people, they go weird on me and I'm back to not understanding them at all. Brother came into the library a few minutes ago demanding that I stop what I was doing and listen to him.

"Fine," I said, Saint Emily the martyr to her father. "But if you get to talk to me, I get to talk to you, too."

"Threats will get you nowhere," Brother said sternly, almost like his old self. He waved a couple of pamphlets under my nose. "I assume I have you to thank for these?"

I made really big eyes and pretended to read the title of the top pamphlet. " 'How to Tell Your Family the Truth.' Hmm. This informative and helpful pamphlet intended to assist old people with how to tell their family horrible news appears to be published by a lung cancer society."

"Yes, it appears that way," Brother said, doing a little teeth-grinding thing that I was very familiar with, having just ground away at least three layers of enamel over Fang's GF. "I found it on my desk."

"On your desk, you say." I batted my lashes at him and put on my most innocent face. "How thoughtful and caring some concerned person is to leave that where it might do some good. Is there something you would like to tell me, Brother?"

"The thoughtful and caring person also left this."

" 'Colon Cancer and You' " I read, cocking an eyebrow.

"And this one." He didn't have enough hair since his last pruning to form the traditional Brother hair horn, but the bit he did have was standing on end like he had stuck his finger in a light socket or something. It kind of melted my heart.

" 'Herpes: One Kiss Can Last for a Lifetime,' " I read out loud. "Um. Perhaps the caring and thoughtful person was figuring it was better to include all possibilities."

"Emily," Brother said, running his hand through his hair stubble. "I don't have cancer."

"Oh. Good." I felt a little bit relieved, but what if he was lying to protect me?

"And I don't have herpes."

"Ah," I said.

"And as for this . . ." He shuffled the pamphlets and held up one. "I appreciate the voiding diary, but I do not suffer from male urinary incontinence, either."

"Good. I didn't want to even think about Mom having to buy you bladder undies," I said with a bright smile.

Despite his almost-return to normalness, his eyes looked tired. "Would you like to tell me why the health fairy felt it necessary to pay me a call?"

"Maybe someone told her that you're not acting normal."

"Normal?" His Unibrow—the one thing I could count on not to change—wrinkled up.

"Well, normal for you, which isn't normal for everyone else, but that's OK; we've learned to live with you."

"Emily," he said with a little sigh, "there's nothing wrong with me. Nothing but . . ."

"But what?" I asked, watching him carefully.

He waved his hands around vaguely, then dropped them. "Nothing. It's nothing. Please, no more pamphlets. I have enough on my mind without you worrying your mother."

Poop! He was going to tell me what was wrong with him; then he changed his mind!

"What do you have on your mind?" I asked, following him to the door as he headed off for the small room in the back of the house he called his office. "If it's not something wrong with your health, what is it?"

"Nothing, Emily," he called back over his shoulder. "It's . . . nothing."

"If you're having an affair, Mom is never going to forgive you," I bellowed after him. "We'll all divorce you, and you'll end up a sad, lonely old man with no one to tell you to comb your hair horn!"

Brother closed the door to his office without saying anything else, which just proves that he is having an affair, don't you think? I mean, he came right out and said it wasn't cancer or colon stuff, but he didn't deny the affair.

Think about it—it makes sense! He's pining away because he's going to have to leave whoever the woman is he's fallen in love with, and he can't tell anyone, so he's moping around not eating, and looking awful, and obviously riddled with great big huge gobs of guilt because he's betrayed Mom's trust. If I didn't feel so sorry for him, I'd say good riddance, but he's not really that bad a guy. Yeah, he's clueless most of the time, but when you really get to know him, he's not that bad a father (with the exception of the fact that he is obsessed with sex when it comes to me dating).

Sigh. Clearly I'm going to have to take care of this situation as well as the Audrey one, Beaky, and the undie ghost.

Oh! Did I tell you about what Mr. Wayne said about my ghost? He came by last night wearing the most bizarre outfit—rainbow-colored pants, tee, and jacket. He looked like some sort of strange, perverted clown, what with his perpetual smile.

"Blessed be all those who dwell within," he said in a dramatic voice when I opened the front door. He made some sort of hand gestures, then came in while I stood blinking at the glare from all that rainbowness. "Good evening, Miss Williams. I see you noticing my garb. This is the first in what I hope will be a long line of chakra wear, clothing I have designed for chakra healers. You will notice that the full spectrum is represented. Good evening, madam, I am Mr. Wayne. You have a very pretty red aura, which I assume means you are this young lady's mother."

Mr. Wayne made a bow as Mom wandered in from another room. She managed to wipe the first look of appalled surprise from her face, which was pretty amazing. I know I was still staring at him like he was a deranged runaway from an extremely sappy kiddie show.

"Um," she said. "Yes, I'm Emily's mother. You must be the gentleman she hired to take care of the haunted underwear drawer."

"The very same. And now, my dear Miss Williams, if I might see the piece of furniture where the entity most frequently resides . . . ?"

"It's upstairs," I said, stepping back so he could go up the stairs first, rolling my eyes at Mom when she slapped a hand over her face so she wouldn't laugh out loud.

Bess came out of her room smelling like incense, wearing a long green velvet dress she called her goddess robe. "Oh, good, is the psychic here? Hi, I'm Bess. I'm Wiccan. I'd love to watch you, if you don't mind. I'm only in my first year of training, so I am not allowed to have any interaction with ghosts, but I'd love to see how you go about exorcising one."

"Exorcise?" Mr. Wayne gasped as I scooted around him and Bess so I could open up my bedroom door. Just as I expected, my undies and bras were all over the room. I felt a bit pervy having Mr. Wayne see them, but figured I'd just have to sacrifice my finer feelings in order to get rid of the ghost. "No, no, no! We do not exorcise! We free. We release. We balance the entity's chakras so he or she is free to fulfill the potential of his or her higher being. But we do not rip them from their connection to the physical plane and throw them out!"

"Oh," Bess said. They came into my room, Mr. Wayne looking around at all the underwear, Bess twirling a finger around the side of her head. I nodded my agreement that he was a bit nutso-cuckoo, and shrugged a further statement that there was nothing I could do.

"Yes, yes, I see. The clothing is scattered everywhere. A classic sign of a troubled entity. We have much work to do here, much work." Mr. Wayne approached the dresser where the underwear ghost lived. "Er . . . which drawer?"

"Top," I said, scooting closer to watch over his shoulder as he opened it. It was empty (it always was).

Mr. Wayne pursed his lips as he carefully pulled the drawer all the way out of the dresser. He examined the drawer carefully without feeling around in it or anything, then set it down and peered into the drawer hole. "Ah, yes, there it is!"

"What? My ghost?" I bent to look, Bess at my side. It just looked like an empty drawer slot.

"Yes, your entity. You see it there, in the left corner?"

I looked. "No."

"Neither do I," Bess said.

"Ah, but you're not looking with your third eye," Mr. Wayne said with a smug smile. "If you open your-

self up to the energies, you'll see it. The entity has man-
ifested itself in a small bluish object somewhat resem-
bling a toad."

"A what?" I stared at him. "I have a blue toad
ghost in my underwear drawer?"

He looked back. "I don't believe he's actually the
ghost of a toad, but rather the entity has taken the
form of a toad."

"He? The ghost was a guy?" Bess asked.

"Oh, yes, most definitely. Male energy is much different from female energy, and this entity is radiating
male energy."

"Why a toad?" I asked. "Why can't it look really
cool, like a handsome guy from a couple hundred
years ago? Like Johnny D in *Pirates of the Caribbean*?
He looked so cool in that movie—not that Orlando
looked bad or anything, because, you know, Orli just
can't look bad, and man, that kiss at the end of the
movie melted my socks, but why does my ghost have
to look like a blue toad instead of a really snogalicious
guy in cool clothes? *Why?*"

"An interesting question, and one that deserves an
answer," Mr. Wayne said after he got through blinking
at me. Old people just never do get Orlando, do they?
"I believe . . ." He paused, pulling on his chin like that
was going to make his brain work better. Who knows,
maybe it does! "I believe we shall have to risk having a
séance in order to communicate with this spirit."

"*Now* you're talking!" I said at the same time Bess

said, "Oooh, yes, a séance! That's just what she needs!"

"Normally I would not risk such an endeavor with an entity so troubled, but in this instance I believe we must first find out in what manner the entity is tormented before I heal his chakras." He pulled a small black date book out of his pocket and consulted it. "I have next Tuesday open, if that would suit. Shall we say midnight?"

"Um . . . I have to get up at six to go to work at the museum. Can we do it earlier?"

His habitual smile dimmed a little bit. "Midnight is the optimal time for a séance. The veil between the physical plane and spiritual one is at its thinnest, and thus communication with those who are caught between the two is easiest."

"Yeah, well, my little toad ghost is just going to have to deal earlier. Seven?"

"Ten," he bartered.

"Eight."

"Nine P.M., and that is the very earliest I am willing to conduct a séance."

"Deal," I said, holding out my hand to shake on it. He looked my hand over like it might have cooties or something before shaking it.

He gave me a little lecture about having pure thoughts and stuff while in my bedroom so I wouldn't contaminate the ghost, then started to put the empty drawer back in the dresser.

"Hey, wait!" I stopped him before he could ram the drawer closed.

"Yes?" he asked.

I waved toward the drawer hole. "You said the ghost was in the back corner. Won't it, like, get squished or something when you put the drawer back?"

"Goddess above, Emily," Bess said, smacking me on the arm. "How ridiculous can you get? It's a ghost. It won't get squished."

I made them leave the drawer out, though. I plan on having a little talk later with the ghost and ask it if it wouldn't please stop being a blue toad and instead turn into Johnny or Orlando or maybe even that hottie Benjamin from *Law and Order* (*he* can haunt my undies anytime!).

So that's what's going on with me! My friend Dru comes tomorrow, but I won't get to see her until after I come home from work. I'll tell you all about our adventures if you tell me what you're doing, other than lying around naked in the sun. (And I agree—tan lines are *so* two hours ago!)

Miss you!
Emily

Subject: Your article in the *Guardian*
From: Emmers@britsahoy.co.uk
To: tmorcale@guardiannews.co.uk
Date: 16 August 2004 10:01 pm

Hi!

My friend Dru saw an article by you in today's newspaper while she and her mom were on the train coming to Piddlington-on-the-Weld to visit my fam and me, and she showed me the article a couple of minutes ago. Can you tell me if when you were doing research into the Black Death and how bubonic plague is making a comeback, you ever found any instances of it in England? I know you said in your article that it was popping up in third-world countries, but Dru and I were thinking, and we wondered if it wasn't possible for Black Death germs to be kind of hibernating on old medieval manuscripts and stuff, just waiting for the right host to come along—someone like a middle-aged man who has bad knees and probably really bad chakras—so it could spawn itself and start a new plague? If you've ever heard of anyone getting the Black Death from a book, could you let me know? I might have another case for you.

Sincerely,
Emily Williams and Dru Chance

Subject: re: Was that you I heard shrieking?
From: Emmers@britsahoy.co.uk
To: Devonator@skynetcomm.com
Date: 16 August 2004 10:09 pm

Devonator wrote:
> *Em, about an hour ago I was at the casino scoping*
> *out the local talent and off in the distance I heard a*
> *strange noise. It was a piercing, screaming sort of*
> *noise, like a cross between a bloke who's caught his*
> *tackle in a vise, and a girl who's just seen a sale sign*
> *at her favorite shoe shop. I reckon that means Dru*
> *has arrived in England?*

Oh, very funny, Mr. Comedian. Yes, she's here. And yes, we screamed. And danced, and hugged each other, and then screamed some more, and cried, and screamed more until Brother said we'd have to stop because our high-pitched yelping (his words, *not* mine) was attracting dogs from five miles away. Don't you dare make fun of us because it's been *eleven whole months* since we've seen each other.

You're just jealous because Fang never screams and dances when you come back from trips.

> *going on with you and Fang? I know you want him*
> *all for your onesie, but Em, don't break him, all*
> *right? He's a good 'un, and I'd hate to see him*
> *strung out because of any bird, and that goes*

> *double when it comes to you. He's in a bad place*
> *now, our Fang is, and I don't want you to make that*
> *worse, even if you mean well.*

Oh, Devon, I wish I knew what to do. I know you think I should let things be, that Fang and Audrey will break up on their own, but I just don't have the time to wait for that! I need her gone now! But I can't think of any way to make her see that she's not right for him, and I won't ask Fang to dump her, because that's just so horrible. You know Fang; he's got the softest heart of anyone I know, and even if he dumped Audrey nicely to be with me, he'd still feel guilty, probably for the rest of his life, and it would ruin everything between us. I'm frustrated and angry and sad and confused and don't know what to do! So I'm doing nothing, which sucks donkey's ears. I hate doing nothing! I'm not a person who likes to sit around and wait for stuff to happen to her. Life is too unreliable to assume everything is going to turn out the way you want it to. Any advice?

Dru sends kisses.
Emily

Subject: Crikey!
From: Emmers@britsahoy.co.uk
To: Devonator@skynetcomm.com
Date: 18 August 2004 11:19 pm

Devonator wrote:
> *That stuff about the ghost is freaky. What happened*
> *at the séance? Did you convince it to dress up like*
> *Johnny Depp? I'll never understand your obsession*
> *with movie stars. Singers are so much cooler. I met*
> *one last night at the casino, a girl named Athena.*
> *She's got a hell of a set of pipes on her.*

Devon! Sheesh, do you have to say something like
that to me? I mean, I know I'm your friend and all,
but geez Louise, I don't talk about guys like that to
you! About their bodies, I mean. I haven't *ever* told
you how cute I think Fang's butt is, and you know
why? Because girls just don't do that! Well, OK, we
talk about butts to each other, but never to a guy!
But hey, if you want to get all palsy-walsy with me
sure, no problem, I can talk butts with you. Fang's
butt is just, like, the *über*-fabu king of all butts. Not
that I've seen it bare-naked, but I've looked when
he's walked away from me, and it's the best butt I've
ever seen. I just want to take great big handfuls of it
and smoosh it around, you know what I mean? It's
buttarific!

Oh. Um. Dru says that pipes means voice and not

boobs, like I thought. Sorry about the butt bit. Just forget you saw it.

The séance was really cool, but before I get to that, Dru wants to say hi.

Hi!

OK, I'm back. We're both majorly PO'd that she only gets to stay with us for three days before her mom drags her off to Wales for two more days, and then they're going back to Seattle, but since her mom used all her frequent-flier miles just so they could come, I guess we can't really complain too much.

We're having loads of fun! I had to go to work on Tuesday because I had not only a big old owl to clean, but also two rush parakeets (oops, sorry, forgot you call them budgies here), so Dru went in with me to keep me company.

She really liked the aid-unit guys who came to resuscitate her.

"Wow, you were right; this place stinks like that possum that got under our bathroom and died. You remember that? Wasn't it awful?" Dru said as I showed her into the cleaning room.

"That was bad, but this is worse." I handed her one of the face masks that didn't do anything about keeping the smell out, but made me feel better anyway. Just the thought of getting bird juice splashed up on my face gave me the heebie-jeebies. "Those are my birds there, in the glass jars."

"Ew. Dead bird bones in a jar. I don't know how

you can stand to do this job, Em, I really don't. It's so rank!"

"It's a job," I said with a shrug, feeling a bit defensive. I mean, it wasn't the greatest job in the world, but it was still a job, and it had some bennies, like being paid in cash at the end of each week. I pulled on a clean pair of rubber gloves and got my tray of cleaning tools. "Look, I have my own scalpel. That's cool, huh? And I have my own desk, and, of course, there's the museum hottie who works with me. So it's not that bad."

"Mmm," Dru said, wrinkling up her nose as I took one of the glass jars and dumped it into the sink so the bird water could drain off. I picked up one of the owl's toes and started scraping away the enamel of its toenail (this is really cool—I found that if you let the toes soak long enough, you can pull the whole toenail casing right off the bone underneath it. It sounds kinda icky, but you'll just have to trust me that it's very slick). Dru watched me for a minute, then started telling me a story about her fiancé Felix, and everything was peachy fuzzy keen until Dru got a bit bored. She started poking around the cleaning room, looking in cupboards, lifting the glass lids off the jars of soaking birds, and even going over to the boiling kettles and asking what was in them.

I told you about the boiling kettles, didn't I? The mammal people use them instead of the beetle room sometimes. I'm not sure why, and I've never, ever looked inside one of the huge kettles that are always simmering away on the counter because although it's bad enough to have to clean a bird skeleton, I wouldn't want to look in the kettle and see a bunny or something boiling away.

"So I said to her, 'Sukie, Em is going to be my maid of honor, because she's my best friend, and we promised each other when we were eight that we were going to be each other's maids of honor,' and then she said that you were all snotty because you'd lived in England for a year, and that you wouldn't talk to anyone when you got back, and then *I* said that you weren't snotty at all, and that she was just jealous because her parents wouldn't let her be an exchange student in Germany. What's in here?"

OK, now, here's the reason I didn't realize right away what had happened: I was at the sink, right? The water was running while I was doing the toenail thing on the owl toesies, and the big overhead fan was going, and although Dru was yelling so I could hear her, she had been going on and on and on about stuff—she talks nonstop sometimes; I don't know how people can stand it—so I was kind of listening to her and cleaning the bird toes and thinking about what we were going to do that night (the séance), and then all of a sudden it struck me that I hadn't heard anything from Dru for a few seconds, so I turned to see what she was doing, and she was flat out on the floor clutching the flat metal lid to one of the boiling kettles.

"Omigod!" I yelled, and dropped the toe I was working on. "Dru! Omigod! What's wrong with you? Dru? Omigod!"

Why is it that you never can remember first-aid stuff when you need it? She was breathing, so I didn't perform CPR on her, but I didn't know what else to do other than yell at her to wake up, so in the end I ran out and got the curator's secretary, and she called the emergency guys, and they came in and revived Dru.

"Monkey heads," she said when they waved something under her nose, and she sat up sputtering and coughing. "Lots and lots of little monkey heads."

"She's delirious," one of the emergency guys said to the other.

"No, she just looked in the boiling kettles," I said sadly, shaking my head as Dru coughed and wheezed. "I told her not to, but would she listen to me?"

The third EMT guy who was standing next to the counter frowned, then leaned over and peered into the kettle, his face going all gray as he saw what was in there.

Now you know why I refuse to look in the boiling kettles.

Anyhoo, Helen, my boss, let us go home early after lunch because Dru refused to stay inside the museum, so we did a little shopping in POTW. Oh! We saw your cousin Tash when we went to Le Grim Morte. Did she tell you they changed the name of the shop again? Anyway, she was all "Aidan and I did this," and

"Aidan said that," which I guess means they're together again. You'd think she'd get a clue, because he's the poster boy for skanky, but she was Little Miss Meow to me, so whatever.

Sorry about calling your cousin a cat, BTW.

The séance was *über*ly fabu. We got to talk to the ghost! Kind of. Oh, OK, Mr. Wayne talked to him, but he told us what the ghost said.

Mr. Wayne came a little before nine. He wasn't wearing his happy clothes—this time he was in dark blue pants and shirt with little moons and stars all over them.

"Those are some bodacious threads," Dru said when Mom sent him up to my room. I made a mental note to tell Dru that no one says *threads* anymore (sometimes she watches way too much MTV), and yelled down the hall for Bess.

Mr. Wayne looked a bit discombobulated for minute, but his smile never dimmed. "Erm . . . thank you. I call this Celestial Moonrise, and it's part of my fashion collection for chakra healers. And you are?"

"Sorry, this is my friend Dru. She's from Seattle, too. She and her mom are staying with us for a couple of days. The oldsters have gone out to hear some medieval poem recited by one of my father's cohorts, which would be totally grotty in itself, but when you consider that I told them they could come to the séance and they chose to hear medieval stuff over finding out who my ghost is, it's just incredible. So do we have to use incense or anything? Bess was in here earlier conducting a ritual cleansing so there wouldn't be any vibes lingering. That won't screw anything up, will it?"

"No, a cleansing is perfectly appropriate. We in the enlightened sphere welcome alternative beliefs and practices by our transcendental brothers and sisters," Mr. Wayne said, baring his teeth in a supersmile at Bess as she came into the room. Between you and me, I think he has the hots for her, which is just *so gross!* I mean, he's got to be *forty!!!*

"It was just a simple cleansing—salt, incense, and ash, to drive away the negative energies Emily spews everywhere," Bess said.

"I do not spew anything, let alone negative energy," I said, outraged. "I'm the most positive-energy person I know. Aren't I the most positive-energy person, Dru?"

"Well—"

"Maybe you don't spew it intentionally, but all that smutty thinking you do while drooling over your latest boy toy has got to have a bad influence. I just cleansed the room of your wicked thoughts, that's all."

"Boy toy! Wicked thoughts! Oh! I'm not the one sleeping with—"

"Ahem," Mr. Wayne said, setting a black bag down on the chair. "Negative energies, ladies! We must avoid all negative thoughts. Now, if Miss Dru could help me with my cloth . . . Thank you."

We spread out a big wide cloth that looked remarkably like an old Halloween tablecloth (it had autumn leaves and black cats on it) on the floor; then Bess lit a bunch of herb candles that she said were supposed to help you make contact with dead people.

"I don't want to make contact with dead people," I said, taking my spot at one side of the tablecloth. Dru was across from me, Mr. Wayne was to my left (facing the dresser), and Bess to my right. "Like I need a bunch of dead people yakking at me? I have enough problems with live people! I just want this ghost gone before we have to leave, because there's no telling how the people who own this house are going to treat him."

"Negative, negative," Bess said as she plopped down.

I stuck my tongue out at her. Dru giggled. Mr. Wayne started swaying and chanting in a funny high-pitched voice. We sat through that for about ten minutes; then suddenly he straightened up and opened his eyes real wide, and said, "We are not alone!"

"It's about time," I muttered, taking a peek at my clock. Dru was making me get up early tomorrow morning so I could jog with her before we went to Manchester. I hate jogging. (It's so stupid! Why run when you can drive somewhere? Swimming is different, but there's no way I ever want to swim with Dru. She almost made the state team this year, and I just know she will next year.)

"Shh!" Bess said, pinching my wrist. I would have pinched her back, but I didn't want to be spewing any more negative energy, so I just gave her the slitty eyes of death.

"There is one here amongst us who has traveled beyond our earthly existence and touched eternity," Mr. Wayne said, his voice kind of flat. So were his eyes, and he wasn't smiling. It was very creepy, Devon! "There is one here who is bound to this place in unholy torment."

"Ask him a question, Em," Dru said in a loud whisper.

The candles—all of them, at the same time!—flickered, just like the ghost had floated through them. I got all goose-bumpy. "Um. Ghost who lives in my underwear drawer, what is your name?"

Mr. Wayne's eyes rolled back in his head and he started swaying again, this time making a strange humming noise. After a couple of sways from side to side, he stopped. "My name is Dermott."

"Kermit?" I asked Dru. "Did he say Kermit? My underwear drawer is haunted by Kermit the frog? Omigod! He's a puppet!"

"Dermott," Mr. Wayne said in his funny voice.

"I think he said *doormat*." Bess was leaning forward to hear Mr. Wayne. "Didn't he say doormat?"

"*Dermott*," Mr. Wayne said louder. "My name is Dermott."

"Dermet? Whoever heard of a name like that?" I asked. I frowned at Mr. Wayne. "How do you spell that?"

"D-E-R-M-O-T-T," he said kind of snappishly, a peeved expression evident in his features.

"Oh. Dermott. Gotcha. Sorry." I made a face at Dru, who had to clap both hands over her mouth to keep from giggling.

Mr. Wayne shot me a quick look, then went back to swaying mode.

"Go on, Emily; ask another question," Bess said, nudging my arm.

"Oh. Um. Dermott, what is your problem with my underwear? It's very nice underwear, and I really don't like having it thrown all around the room, so if you could just tell me what the problem is, maybe we could work out a time-share situation with the undie drawer."

Mr. Wayne hummed and swayed for a bit, then stopped suddenly again. "I died in this room."

"Ew!"

"Shh!" Bess frowned at me.

"Double *ew* with knobs on it!"

"Shh!"

"Don't *shh* me; you didn't have someone die in your room!"

"Emily, if you don't be quiet, the ghost will leave Mr. Wayne and you won't find out what his problem is. Ask him what he died of."

"Where did you die, Dermott? Was it in the bed? Because if you died in the bed, I'm never sleeping in it again!"

121

Bess sighed. "Don't be stupid! It wouldn't be the same bed!"

"How do you know? Were you here when Dermott died?"

Dru giggled.

Mr. Wayne made an annoyed sound and I stopped glaring at Bess to look at him. "I died of fright when I was cursed by the Almighty with a rain of toads."

"Aha!" I said, feeling just like Sherlock Holmes. Only without the pipe. "Toads! That's significant!"

"A rain of toads?" Dru asked. "That's biblical! I heard about that from Father Tom. He said that God smote people with toads in ancient times."

"Dermie, just when exactly did you die?" I asked Mr. Wayne.

Sway, sway, hum, hum. "In the year of our Lord seventeen hundred and eighty-eight."

"No!"

Dru and I stared at each other, both our mouths hanging open for a few seconds before we reached across the candles to high-five each other. *Pirates of the Caribbean*!" we both yelled.

"Oh, Goddess," Bess said, covering her eyes.

"Dermie, you have to, you know, show yourself right now. Because we absolutely love the clothes that guys wore back then."

"Totally!" Dru said. "Do you have long black hair with beads and things tied into it?"

"Or a ponytail? Ponytails are so cool!"

Dru looked at me, her eyes huge. "Braids in his beard!"

"Eeeeeeeeeek!" I screamed.

"Oh, Goddess, oh, Goddess, oh, Goddess," Bess moaned, her hands still over her eyes as she started rocking back and forth.

"You have to make him show himself," I told Mr. Wayne, who was sitting still with a kind of horrified look on his face. "I demand that he show himself. It's my ghost, right? I can do that, can't I? As the hauntee, I have certain rights, don't I?"

"Erm—"

"Dermott! I command you to . . . uh . . ." I leaned to the side. "Psst. Bess. What's the word?"

"Manifest," she said, still moaning.

"As your hauntee, I demand you manifest in front of us right now!"

"Erm . . ." Mr. Wayne said.

"Come on, Dermott, we want to see you," Dru said. "Don't be shy! We like boys!"

"Oooh. Thought." I gnawed on my lip for a few seconds. "Maybe he's old and creepy like—" I glanced at Mr. Wayne and stopped. "Maybe he's old and creepy and we don't want to see him?"

"Ask him," Dru said.

"Good idea. Dermott, are you a hottie or a nottie?"

"Goddess above, Emily! You can't speak to a spirit that way! It's disrespectful."

I pointed my finger at Bess. "You take all the fun

123

out of having a ghost. OK, Dermott, rephrase: How old were you when you died?"

Mr. Wayne was looking down at his hands like he was trying to sneak a peek at his watch. "Er . . . oh. Mmmmm . . ." He started humming again, jerked a couple of times as if he were being electrocuted, then said, "I died in my prime. I was naught but five and twenty."

I narrowed my eyes at Dru. She made squishy lips back at me as we thought that over.

"Kinda old. Felix is only nineteen."

"Yeah, but Fang is twenty. I like older men."

She frowned. "But twenty-five—that's eight years older than us."

"But still well within the hottie range," I pointed out.

"That's it!" Bess said, getting to her feet. "I'm leaving. I will not stand around and watch you two heathens insult a spirit this way. Enjoy your séance."

"Hey, you can't leave before Dermott manifests! What if he's hideous and pus-covered and gross?"

Bess paused at the door. "What good would I be if he was?"

I grinned at her. "You can scare him away!"

"Oh, for God's . . . Goddess's sake . . ." Bess slammed the door behind her as she left, which was a bit of a bummer because it brought Mr. Wayne out of his trance or altered state or whatever it was he was in to channel Dermott the ghost.

We tried to talk him into hanging around and giving it another shot, but he said he had to do a polter-geist check at another house and he couldn't stay.

"But what am I supposed to do?" I asked as I fol-lowed him down the stairs. "All I know is that my ghost's name is Dermott, he's twenty-five, and he was killed by a rain of toads in my bedroom."

Mr. Wayne paused by the front door while I dug through my purse and got the money for the séance. He spoke really hurriedly, like he couldn't wait to get away. "The entity who resides in your room is deathly afraid of toads due to the manner in which he died. In order to free him from the torment that grips him and keeps him bound to the earthly plain, you must re-lease him of his fear."

"What? Release him of his fear? How do I do that?"

"Toads," Mr. Wayne said, snatching the money out of my hand and stuffing it in his pocket before start-ing for the door.

"Toads? You mean I'm supposed to put a toad in the dresser?"

"Not one." Mr. Wayne stood in the middle of the open door and smiled a slow, evil smile. "As many as you can find. Hundreds of toads, thousands of toads. You must fill your room with toads in order to over-come the entity's fear of them."

"You are out of your friggin' mind!" I said with a full-frontal goggle.

His smile got bigger. "It is the only way. If you really wish to release this entity, you must first cure him of his unnatural fear of toads. Fill the room with them! Then call me for another séance and we'll send him on to his spiritual reward."

Dru and I watched with stunned looks on our faces (I checked in the mirror in my purse—I looked as stunned as she did) as he left.

The door closed with a soft *shooft* sound. Dru blinked at the door for a couple of minutes, then turned to me. "Where are you going to find a roomful of toads?"

"I don't know," I said, still stunned. "Maybe a pet shop? *Toads?* He wants me to fill the room with *toads?*"

"Well," Dru said as we started back up the stairs toward my Dermott-haunted room, "all I can say is it's a good thing I'm leaving in two days, because toads are just totally freaky."

"Toads," I said again, and wondered why my life always had to be like something out of Bizarro Land.

Pooh, I have to go again. It seems like I always have so much to tell you, but not enough time to type it all up. But that won't matter once you come home. Yay, it's only five more days!

Smoochies!
Emily

Subject: Flash!
From: Emmers@britsahoy.co.uk
To: Devonator@skynetcomm.com
Date: 19 August 2004 7:16pm

You are not going to believe this—Holly and Ruaraidh have broken up! I know, I'm shocked too! Holly is in tears, so it's kind of hard to understand her, but I gather that Ruaraidh called her up and told her he wants a girlfriend whom he can see more than once every two months, and then she said something about him being able to see her more often if he didn't go to a football game every weekend, and then he said that she was stifling him, and she said that he wasn't thinking about her feelings at all, and it all went downhill after that.

Poor Holly. Poor Fang and me. Poor everyone.

Gotta run so I can call Holly back and see if she's stopped crying yet.

Hugsies!
Emily

Subject: You're lucky I don't have a potty mouth!
From: Emmers@britsahoy.co.uk
To: randrews@alba21century.co.uk
Date: 19 August 2004 7:17pm

You are the biggest poop on the planet, Ruaraidh, and I formally defriend you.

Just so you know!

Emily

Subject: re: You're better than that American entertainment channel
From: Emmers@britsahoy.co.uk
To: Devonator@skynetcomm.com
Date: 20 August 2004 7:16pm

> *I'm sorry that Holly was crying so hard she blew all*
> *over her mum's new carpet. I have to say that your*
> *detailed, leave-nothing-out account of her vomiting*
> *made me feel like I was right there with you. That's*
> *one of the things I love about you, Emily—you don't*
> *want your friends to feel out of touch with what's*
> *going on in your life.*

I am so totally bummed. Nothing has gone right for the last couple of days. I'm going to tell you all about it, too, and if you lip off to me about telling you stuff,

I will punish you. And you can stop with that naughty grin I know you're wearing, because I'm not going to spank you or anything kinky like that. No, my punishment for you will be much, much worse.

I'll make you take me shoe shopping.

Let's see, where should I start? Holly, first, since I left you in the middle of her ralphing. She's doing better now, although I got a very snarky e-mail from Ruaraidh telling me to mind my own business. I forwarded it to Holly, and she got all mad at him, and that made her feel a whole lot better, although I'm a bit worried—she wants to date one of the guys at the camp she works at (oh, before I forget, you are still planning on wearing your knight stuff and helping us with Helm's Deep? I'm counting on you to be Aragorn! I'm going to be Éowyn, except I won't be hiding in a cave; I'm going to be out there fighting. I've even got a wooden sword I'm practicing with. Um. Where was I?) . . . and you know I'm normally all for the "get right back in the dating saddle after you've been dumped" policy, but Holly is different from most girls. She's more delicate emotionally.

The thing is, she's not listening to me! I used to be able to advise her, so she would avoid things that I knew she shouldn't do, but then Ruaraidh came into the picture, and my aunt Tim said I had to let her make her own mistakes, and I did because I hate it when people tell me I'm doing something wrong.

"Hol, you know you're my best friend," I said to her after she called me up to tell me how mad she was at seeing Ruaraidh's e-mail to me.

"Next to Dru, yes, I know."

"No, not next to Dru, alongside Dru," I said, and was kind of surprised because I meant it. "You're both my best friends. And just like I don't want Dru to be hurty and stuff, I don't want you to make yourself miserable when there's no reason to. You're on the rebound, and rebound relationships never work out. I know you think Craig is dishy and all, and I agree that any guy who is willing to play Legolas has got to be a quality hottie, but you can take it from me that you're heading for disaster city."

"I don't see why you say that," Holly said, a bit defensively. "Just because your love life is in shambles doesn't mean mine has to be!"

It was on the edge of my tongue to say that my relationships were adult ones and hers were just crushes, but I didn't. Oh, I wanted to! I really wanted to! I opened my mouth three times to say it, but I didn't because I knew that it would hurt her more than she had just hurt me. Aren't you proud of me? I didn't even tell her what she should do; I just said, "You're right, Hol. It's none of my beeswax what you do. If you want to go out with Craig, then do it."

I kind of half thought she'd say she was sorry then and ask my advice about the situation, but she didn't.

She just said that she'd been doing a lot of thinking about her life, and she thought it was time to stand up for what she wanted. So I guess that's good, but it makes me feel like crying a little. Holly has always been so needy, you know, so gentle and easily hurt by people, and now she's talking about dating a guy only two days after she broke up with her longtime BF.

It's like she doesn't *need* me anymore.

So that's the first bad thing that happened. Then Dru left, which was sad, and we cried, and hugged each other, and cried some more, and used up a whole box of Kleenex.

Brother is still being weird. He's either having an affair or he's become an international medieval antiquities thief and he's worried about getting caught smuggling stuff he stole through customs. There's just no other explanation for his moodiness. I'm going to drop by his office in Oxford and see what's going on. I bet there's some hot young secretary somewhere telling him he has to leave his wife and family.

Oh, no, what if he's having a midlife crisis? Dru's dad had one of those, and he divorced her mom and got himself a shiny red Porsche and a trophy wife! Eeek! Must go find out who this evil woman is and tell her Brother is too old for a Porsche!

As if all that weren't enough, I got yelled at at work, today, too. I worked only half a day because Dru was leaving in the morning, and Helen said I could work late, but then I got yelled at and sent home because—and I swear to you this wasn't my fault! I shut the door, I know I did—the beetles got out of the beetle room, and were all over the metal filing cabinets holding the stuffed birds, which means they have to spray all the filing cabinets with bug spray in case some beetles got into them.

"Do you have any idea how much damage those beetles could do?" Helen yelled, pointing a finger at one of the cabinets. "They could destroy the entire collection!"

"I'm sorry," I said for the gazillionth time. "But I'm sure I closed both doors. I always do, because otherwise the stink gets out."

"No one else was working in that area but you," Helen said. At least she'd stopped yelling by then. I stood there feeling miserable while everyone—the Chrises and Sam and Kia and Brent and a couple of secretaries—ran around stomping on beetles.

"I know I closed the door," I said again, wishing I could just quit, but I need the money because I'm trying to save to buy Fang a ticket to Seattle.

"Maybe it was the ghost," Brent suggested as he whapped his hand down on the top of a case, wiping smooshed beetle off on the edge. "Harry does mischievous things all the time. He mucked up the skinning room a couple of months ago. Perhaps he decided to free the beetles?"

"So funny I forgot to laugh," I told Brent, which I admit wasn't very nice, but he got all shirty with me and wouldn't help squash beetles after that. Honestly, I didn't even want to think about the beetle incident being due to another ghost. I have enough problems with just the one!

And speaking of that, when Helen sent me home early I went to the pet shop on High Street and asked about toads. The woman there said they didn't have any toads, but they had some frogs that evidently they keep for a customer who has a couple of big frog-eating snakes. So I bought those and then I had to buy an aquarium and frog stuff to keep them, because I can't just let them die in my room. (That's all I need—the ghosts of frogs haunting me.) It took all the rest of my money to buy the frog food and light and all that stuff, and I'm not even sure they'll work!

"What exactly is the difference between a toad and a frog?" I asked the pet-store lady as I looked at the three frogs she put in a little box. The only good thing about my getting them was that they wouldn't be dinner for some snake.

"Toads are actually like frogs, but there are some differences between the two species. For instance, toads tend to have warty, dry skins, whereas frogs have smooth and slimy skins because they prefer wetter environments. Toads also have stubbier bodies, and shorter back legs, where frogs have very strong back legs for hopping rather than walking."

"I just hope Dermott doesn't know the difference," I said under my breath as I walked off with my aquarium full of frog stuff.

I don't know how Mr. Wayne thinks I'm supposed to fill my room with toads in just a couple of weeks, but the three frogs, which, BTW, I've named Nat, Dylan, and Alex (*Charlie's Angels,* get it?), are just going to have to do the job, because I can't afford to buy any more!

That's my whole horrible day. Please, please, please tell me what's up with you. Fang took Audrey to Brighton for a couple of days, and I'm so miserable I could scream.

Emily

Subject: re: We're back!
From: Emmers@britsahoy.co.uk
To: Dru@seattlegrrl.com
Date: 22 August 2004 5:18pm

Dru wrote:
> *miss you so much! I know you like England and*
> *your friends, but I will be glad when you come*
> *home. It was so much fun seeing you again! Felix*
> *came by last night and brought me flowers because*
> *he went crazy while I was gone. Isn't that sweet?*
> *He's just the sweetest honey-bunny there ever was.*

Very sweet. I wasn't too sure he was the right guy for you, but after that night we sat up until two talking about guys and you told me how he's willing to quit school to support you and everything, well, I've changed my mind. It does sound like he's the perfect Mr. Dru, and you're lucky that you found him.

You know, I hadn't really thought about going home. Oh, I have, but you know what I mean. I thought about it, not really *thought* about it. But now I have and . . . Oh, man, Dru, why is my life always so sucky? If I stay here—not that Brother would let me—I'd miss seeing you and everyone back home. If I go home, I won't get to see Fang and Holly and Devon. It's so not fair! I wish Brother had never dragged us to England! I hate this!

~Em

Subject: Sorry
From: Emmers@britsahoy.co.uk
To: Dru@seattlegrrl.com
Date: 22 August 2004 6:59pm

OK, I'm insane, I admit it. I'm sorry about that last e-mail. I just got so sad thinking about everything that I kind of lost it there for a few minutes. But I'm still determined to be intelligent and proactive, not because I have to fight for Fang, but because intelligent and proactive is just a whole lot better than whiny and miserable. Besides, I have to make Brother understand that he wouldn't like a Porsche and a trophy wife, and deal with all the rest of the crap that makes up my life, and there's no way I can do that while sniveling.

So no more whinging. From here on out, I'm not going to whinge one single solitary . . . um . . . whinge. It's just going to be proactive intelligent Emily all the way.

I spent the day with Fang and Audrey. Yeah, I know, thrillsville—a day spent with my boyfriend-who-isn't-my-boyfriend and his girlie-girl who is turning out to *not* be the evil BF-stealing girl I want her to be. It's horrible, Dru, but I'm actually starting to like her! I want to hate her! She's standing between me and Fang! But she's not that bad once you get to know her.

We went to see a movie—*Catwoman* again, since they hadn't seen it—and then Fang drove us up to Stratford-upon-Avon to see the Shakespeare stuff (Audrey likes that kind of thing). It was kind of fun to look around the old houses that Anne Hathaway (Mrs. Shakespeare) and William's mom lived in—everything was *über*-Ye Olde Englande there—but it was also frustrating as heck.

"Wow, look at him. Hottie Central," I'd say upon spotting a cool-looking guy whom I thought Audrey would like.

"Mmm," she'd answer, and would grab Fang's

hand, which made me grind my teeth. Fang looked like he was doing the same, although I noticed he never once pried her hand off his.

sigh I'm doing it again. Ignore that hand-prying comment. I didn't mean it. (Well, I did, but I don't like to admit that I did, because if Fang was the type of guy to two-time his GF, I wouldn't like him, so it doesn't matter, if you know what I mean.)

"Mmmrowr!" I purred later as we were having lunch outside a pub called the Dirty Duck (supposed to be famous, although it just looked Ye Olde to me). I nudged Audrey's arm and pointed to a really scrummy guy in bike shorts who walked his bike past us. "Check him out! Buns ahoy!"

"Nice, but not as nice as what I already have," she said, grinning at Fang. He looked like he was going to be sick, although he did manage to smile back at her. A sick smile.

"Hoo, baby, twins at twelve o'clock!" I said an hour later as we were walking along the Avon (it's the river there). Two guys were walking toward us, not gorgeous enough to make me drool, but they looked like Audrey's type. "Hey, guys, if you could have your pick, which one would you choose?"

Fang looked at me like I was crazy.

"Well, OK, you don't have to pick, but Audrey, which one would you choose?"

"Oh . . . probably the one on the left," she said,

137

giving the guys a quick glance before stopping to coo over some baby ducks floating near the riverbank.

"Left, huh? I would have gone for the one on the right, but that's just me," I muttered under my breath as I headed straight for the twins. Fang started to give me an odd look as I left, but had to stop when Audrey pulled him over to look at the duckies.

"Hi," I said, stopping right in front of the twin hotties (twotties? Ahahahahahaha!). Maybe they weren't twins, but they must have been brothers, because they looked a lot like each other. "I'm Emily. I'm American. My friend Audrey—she's the one over there bending over to look at the baby ducks—is from New Zealand. She thinks you're really hot," I said to the twin on the left. "I don't suppose you'd like to show her around town, huh? I'm sure she'd love it, because she's very into history and touristy stuff, and she's really nice. Hey, I have an idea—why don't you *both* show her around?"

The twins looked at each other, then back at me. "Bwa bwab waabwa wbawabwa," one of them said. Honest, he sounded just like the Swedish Chef on *The Muppet Show*!

"Oh, great, you don't speak English?"

"Bwabwa bwawbwabwa bwaaaaa," the second twin said.

I grabbed the arm of the left twottie, and yelled over to where Audrey and Fang were. "Hey, Aud! These guys are Swedish or something and they think you're cool beans! They want to show you around the town. Isn't that slick?"

"Bwa bwah?" one of the twins asked the other.

"Bwah bwa bwahah Yulia Roberts," the other said, pointing at Audrey.

I smiled at them as I dragged them over to the riverbank. "Yeah, she does kind of look like Julia, huh? Julia? Looks like Julia? Ya, sure, you betcha!"

"Ja, ja." The twins laughed. "Yulia Roberts."

"Audrey, these guys are just wild to meet you and show you around Stratford," I said as we pulled up. "You're all they can talk about! This one . . . Um . . . what was your name?"

Twottie number one just looked at me.

"Oh, well, you can find out their names while they show you around the place," I said, giving Audrey a little push toward the two guys. They laughed and each took one of her hands, *bwa bwa bwa*-ing like mad at her.

"But . . . but . . ." she said as they hauled her up the river path toward the main part of town, looking over her shoulder at us. "But, Fang—"

"Oh, don't worry," I said, slipping my arm through Fang's. "I'll take care of him while you're seeing everything. Have fun!"

"That was incredibly subtle," Fang said, watching as the twotties and Audrey disappeared into the crowd.

"I'm known for my subtlety," I said, smiling at him.

He tried to look stern and mad, like he didn't appreciate what I had done, but the corners of his mouth smiled, so I knew he wasn't really.

We spent a wonderful half hour walking along the river, talking about stuff—everything but Audrey (I didn't want to waste the little time I had)—but when we came back into town, I knew nothing had changed. In fact, it was worse.

"I guess this was a stupid idea, huh?" We were stopped on a narrow footbridge, staring down into the river as it swooshed beneath us. On the other side of the river, near a pub that looked out over the river, Audrey stood with the Swedish guys. "I keep trying to pretend that it's going to get better, but it doesn't, does it?"

Fang stood next to me, his fingers touching mine as we looked at the water. He sighed a long sigh. "I'm going to tell her. I can't go on like this anymore, Emily. It's not fair to any of us."

I looked over to where Audrey was standing. Although the twins were yakking at her a mile a minute, she was watching us. Or rather, she was watching Fang. And I knew then, right at that moment, that all my intelligent proactivism wasn't going to do any good. I could fight for Fang all I wanted, but all it was going to do would be to make us all miserable. And I was already about as miserable as I could get. I hated to think of making everyone else feel that way.

"We're flying home at the end of the month," I said, my heart breaking into a gazillion little pieces.

"I know," Fang said, brushing his thumb over my nearest finger. "I'm going to take a second job so I can visit you."

I shook my head, watching as the brown water of the river flowed under the stone bridge. It's weird, but when you see a river from a distance, it looks like it's just one color—brown, gray, black, whatever. But when you look at it really close, you can see all sorts of other things that make it up—little sticks floating on the surface, bubbles sometimes, bits of paper, that sort of thing. Separate bits on their own, but they smoosh together to make the river. I looked at that river and I knew that what I had been seeing as just one thing was really made up of all sorts of elements.

I wanted Fang all to myself, but I hadn't thought about what he wanted. Even if I did get Audrey to leave in a way that wouldn't leave Fang (and me) feeling horribly guilty, then where would we be? He'd be in England, and I'd be in Seattle. Even if we both worked so he could fly out to see me, he couldn't stay for long. It would always be short visits; then he'd have to go home to England again. He'd be here, alone, lonely, with no girlfriend because I know he'd never two-time me, and we'd see each other only a couple of times a year. He'd have his life, and I'd have mine.

Audrey liked him. He liked Audrey. If I hadn't been

there to mess things up, they would probably be pretty happy together.

It all came down to whether or not I was selfish enough to want him for myself without thinking of what was best for him.

"No," I said, ignoring the fact that the gazillion pieces of my broken heart were being crushed into dust. "Don't bother. It's not worth it. It's over before it even started."

"Emily," he said, grabbing my hand as I started to walk past him.

It hurt too much to look him in the eye, so I looked at his ear (the most adorable ear in the world) instead. "Don't, Fang. We just weren't meant to be together, I guess. It's kind of like Romeo and Juliet, only not nearly so sappy, and neither one of us has to talk funny or drink poison."

"Don't say that, Em." His voice, always so wonderful, was filled with hurt. It plucked at me, making me want to throw myself in his arms and beg him to make everything happy again. "Don't say that we don't have a future. I don't mind getting a second job. I'll see you as often as I can—"

"Once every couple of months?" I asked, suddenly angry. Why was he making this so hard? I was willing to do the self-sacrificing thing and give him up, and he was being a poop and not letting me be noble and all! "I'm sorry, Fang. It's not good enough. I love you, but it's just not good enough. I want a full-time boyfriend, not one who is only there a couple of times a year."

He let go of my hand and I walked off—I just walked away and left him standing on that stupid bridge. It was just like something out of one of those weepy chick movies, only a hundred times worse. And it hurt. It hurt so much I thought seriously about running away from them and finding my own way home, but you know me; I'm always the one to face stuff until the grim end.

And boy, was this end grim.

I didn't even cry as I passed Audrey (she went off to see Fang); I just marched off to Fang's car and sat on the hood until they came back. Fang looked awful, and only once met my eyes. The look in his puppy-dog eyes made me feel the worst I'd ever felt, like I'd killed something inside of him. I wanted to yell at him that something inside of me had died, too, but I didn't. I didn't even call shotgun—I just got into the back of the car and pretended to sleep all the way home.

That's it. That's what happened. I've made my decision—yeah, I know, I keep changing my mind about what to do about Fang, but this time it's final—and I'm going to stick to it.

So here's the new game plan:

1. I'm going to forget Fang. I can do it. And if I can't, I'll have Bess hypnotize me into forgetting him.

2. I'm going to forget Holly. Since she's obviously just dine and fandy without me, I won't feel the least little bit bad about leaving her.

3. I'm going to forget Dermott, too. He's still throwing my underwear around the room, although he only did about half my things, rather than everything in the drawer. I wonder if I should put the frogs in the drawer with him rather than have them on top? You know, kind of like shock therapy. Hmmm. Will think on it.

4. I'm going to go right up to Brother and tell him to knock off whatever it is he's doing. I'm tired of worrying about him, too, and I refuse to do it anymore!

5. I'm going to take Beaky to the vet to see if she can do a beak transplant on him. Holly said she would take the birds when we leave, so at least I won't have to find them a new home, but I hate to leave her with a handicapped bird. Not that I care what she thinks, you understand. It's all about the bird.

6. I'm going to finish out my time at work, and won't say anything about the possibility that someone left the beetle doors open just to make me look bad. I mean, why would anyone do that?

7. I'm going to stop crying.

I feel better now that I have a new plan. Devon comes home tonight. I think I'll go over to his house and welcome him back. He's the only one I won't forget about.

Squeezies and smooches,
~Em

Subject: That's it!
From: Emmers@britsahoy.co.uk
To: Dru@seattlegrrl.com
Date: 22 August 2004 10:46pm

I told Devon what happened with you-know-who, and he asked me to be his girlfriend again.
   I'm officially forgetting *everyone* in England!
   I can't wait to come home.

~Em

Subject: re: OMG!!!!
From: Emmers@britsahoy.co.uk
To: Dru@seattlegrrl.com
Date: 24 August 2004 7:50pm

Dru wrote:
> it!!! I can't believe you broke it off with Fang! I
> can't believe you were so selfless! Emily, that was
> just like a saint or something, sacrificing your love
> for his happiness. OMG, I'm going to cry just thinking

> about it! You are so amazing! I could never give
> Felix up. I'd die if I did! But you're putting Fang's
> feelings totally ahead of yours, and that's just so . . .
> so . . . noble!!!

I don't know what you're talking about, Dru. I don't know anyone named Fang.

Today was rotten at work. Brent was teasing me because I told Sam and Chris L about Dermott, and now he says I see dead people and keeps asking me to read his palm. Helen is still mad about the beetles, and Chris G, whom I flirted with at lunch, asked me if I wanted to go see a movie with him (*Catwoman . . .* how many times can I see it without actually going insane?). I said yes, of course, because I'm not stupid, and it's not like I have a BF or anything. So we're going Friday night. I asked him if he wanted to come to the Helm's Deep thing on Saturday (I have to do it even though I don't want to anymore), and he said he might, so that's good. It would be nice to have someone there that I like.

The worst thing about work was what happened when I came in. I got there early because I'm trying to make up the time I missed while you were here, and so there was no one in the back offices. I toddled past the cases (now beetle-free again, and just so it's perfectly clear, none of the stuffed birds were eaten), and into the little office that I share with Helen, dropping off my things. Then I went back into the area formerly known as the lunchroom, and what did I see but a big metal barrel in the middle of the room with tall red things sticking out of it. I went closer to see what they were, but not too close, because after the monkey head incident . . . well, 'nuff said, right? Anyhoo, I couldn't figure out what they were, so I just made coffee and went back into the office.

An hour later the two Chrises and Sam came in.

"What's this?" Chris G asked.

"I don't know. I didn't want to look too closely at it," I called through the open doorway.

They all circled the big barrel, squinting at the tall red things.

"I know what it is—it's Princess!" Chris L finally said.

"Princess? Princess who?" I asked, wondering if the museum was starting to collect dead humans now. *Ew!*

"Princess the giraffe at the zoo. Didn't you hear about it? She died and we managed to get her body. Excellent! We'll have to do our prep work now. These legs are too long to fit into the freezers."

Ew, ew, ew! Dead giraffe legs! I had been in the same room as dead giraffe legs! OMG!

Because I am the new *über*-cool Emily, I didn't run screaming from the room. I just sat there and pretended that none of them were there, and avoided that room for the rest of the day until the legs were gone. I didn't even drink the coffee I'd made because it was in the same room as *dead giraffe leg germs!!!*

> *also can't believe that Devon wants you as his GF*
> *again! He must really be in love with you, Em. Are*
> *you going to take him up on it? He's rich enough*
> *that he could come see you a lot, so you wouldn't*
> *have to miss him like you would Fang.*

I'm sorry, I don't understand what you're talking about. I don't know anyone named Devon, either. In fact, I don't . . . Oh, poop, Brother wants me. BRB.

That's it, I give up, I just give up trying. I give up trying to stay sane; I give up trying to be happy. No one wants me to be either, so I'll just be insane and unhappy, and then everyone else will be happy, because that's all that matters, isn't it?

Gah!

Brother dragged me into his office, which is always a bad thing because it means he wants to have a serious talk.

"I don't suppose you want to have a talk about what sort of antiquities you're planning on smuggling home," I asked as I followed him into his room.

He stopped in the doorway and frowned. "What? What antiquities? Who is smuggling antiquities?"

I waved it away. "No one. Never mind. So who's the babe at work that you're preparing to dump Mom and us over?"

His jaw dropped as he flopped down into the beat-up leather chair that he loves. He stared at me for a minute like I had a blue toad on my head; then his eyes narrowed. "All right, missy. Just what are you on? Marijuana? Crack? Heroin?"

I rolled my eyes. "I'm not on anything, Brother. I'm just tired of people playing games with me. Who's the woman?"

He leaned back in his chair, cartwheeling his arms and legs as the chair almost tipped over backward (it's missing a spring or something in the back), pulling himself upright to glare at me. "There is no other woman, Emily."

"Well, then, what is it? What's making you act so weird?"

"Weird how?" he asked, his eyes still doing the narrow thing at me.

"You know, *weird!*"

"Ah. Weird, perchance, as in moody?"

"Yeah, moody. You've been very moody. Very depressed."

"Walking around with a long face?" he asked.

"Exactly."

"And perhaps also not taking pleasure in the things one normally takes pleasure in?"

"Yeah!" I shook my finger at him. "Mom says you haven't been eating a lot. And you don't yell at me like you normally do. That's just weird."

"I see," he said in his professor's voice, one half of his Unibrow cocked upward. "You didn't notice yourself that I haven't been eating as normal?"

I waved that question away. "No, I've had a bit of a

stomach thing. Summer flu, I think. I haven't felt much like food."

"Mmm. I notice you haven't asked me for money lately, either, or nagged me to take you places, or pestered me with your problems."

"It's called growing up, Brother," I said very maturely. "I don't run to my daddy with my problems anymore. And I'm working now, so I don't need any money."

"Pity," Brother said, rubbing his chin. "I always rather enjoyed being pestered by you. You always had such a fertile mind when it came to squeezing me for money."

"So what's up, then?" I asked, ignoring his comment. "What's wrong with you?"

He smiled at me; he actually smiled at me. Oh, it was a sad smile, but it was still a smile. I always worry when Brother smiles at me. It's *so* not him! "We are so much alike that it's almost frightening. Bess is truly your mother's daughter, but you . . . ah, Emily, you have more of me in you than your much more level-headed mother. You share my academic curiosity, a single-minded determination that makes us happiest when we are pursuing a goal, and what I fear is an emotional state that tips toward passion rather than placidity. In short, daughter mine, what troubles me is the same thing that troubles you—I regret having to leave England and return home. Like you, I will deeply miss the friends I have made here, and also like you, I am mourning them even before we have left."

"You're wrong about that," I said, surprised to find I was crying. The tears just seemed to appear without my even thinking about them. Brother handed me a box of tissues without saying anything. "I want to go home. I don't care about anyone here. I can't wait to go back . . . back . . ."

"It hurts, doesn't it, sweetling?" He came around to the big overstuffed armchair I was in and sat on the arm, pulling me up against him. "I wish we could be different, Em, but we are as we are. We love wholly, we hate deeply, and we feel everything passionately. Your mom and Bess have it easier. They really are looking forward to going home, but you and I . . . Your young man, your boyfriend, came to see me today. He said you're not talking to any of your friends. He said that Holly has called every day for the last four days, and you won't talk to her. He said you've cut everyone off."

"I don't have a boyfriend," I said, sniffling into the tweed of Brother's jacket. He loved tweed. He loved wearing English tweed jackets with leather patches on the elbow. He loved talking in a fake English accent. He loved all the castles, and the people, and the food. He loved everything about England. Just that thought made me cry harder.

"Well, I'm certainly not going to be the one to push you into a romantic relationship, but from what the young man said, it seems he does feel strongly about you."

151

I thought about denying everything. We were leaving in less than a week—I could hold out against Brother's questioning for that long. But in the end, Dru, I didn't. Do you know how long it's been since I cried on Brother? It was when I was twelve and Mimsy died. I loved that cat so much, and when she died, I thought I was going to die, too. Kind of like how I feel now. "I'm being noble. I'm giving him up because we don't have a future together. I'm thinking about him instead of me, OK? So can we quit with the third degree, because my nose is running, and I hate anyone seeing me with a stuffed-up, runny nose."

His arm tightened around me. "Emily, I'm going to give you a very sage piece of advice. I don't expect you'll follow it, because you've never followed any advice I've given you yet, but regardless, I'm going to give it to you in hopes that it might ease the path you are so determined to forge for yourself."

"If you're going to tell me that I shouldn't pretend that my friends don't exist—"

"No," he said, lifting my chin so he could look me in the eye. "My advice is simply this—be happy."

I snarfed. "That's it? That's your big father/daughter-talk advice? That's all there is to it?"

He nodded. "That's it. Do what makes you happy. Life is too short to spend it regretting that you didn't do something you wanted to do. If there's one thing I've learned, it's that no matter how many obstacles there may seem to be in your life, if you are happy, you will overcome them."

"What if it would make me happy to rob a bank?" I said, still sniffing in an attempt to breathe through my nose again.

"Would it make you happy to rob a bank?" he asked.

"No, but what if it would?"

"Then I would expect you to become the world's best, most successful bank robber."

I grabbed another tissue and sat back in the chair. "I hate my life."

He nodded and pushed a strand of hair off my forehead. "I know. It's not easy being seventeen." He sang the words to the tune of "It's Not Easy Being Green."

I couldn't help but laugh. "You're insane, Brother."

He grinned as he went over to his chair. "I know, but you love that about me."

I played with a tissue for a few minutes, then looked up. "Nothing has changed, though. It's fine for you to say, 'Be happy,' but I'm not happy."

He picked up his reading glasses and a paper he was proofing. "Then I expect you'll have to change whatever it is you're doing."

"That's easy for you to say."

"Mmm." He ignored me for the paper.

I got up and went to the door, pausing when he said, "Oh, Emily?"

"You're not going to go all mushy on me and say that you're proud of me no matter what I do, and you'll always love me, and you know life is hard, but it's what you make of it, and all that, are you?" I asked. "Because if you do, I'm going to have to scream."

His Unibrow rose in horror. "Good Lord, I would never say anything so wholly emotional and completely appalling."

I smiled at him. There were times when I really liked my father. There were other times when he drove me mad, but this was one of the good times. "What were you going to say?"

His jaw worked for a second before he spoke. "Ostriches get eaten."

"Huh?" Obviously the emotional strain of our little bonding session had been too much for his mind. He'd snapped. A lot.

He nodded. "You heard what I said. Go on; I have work to do."

I have to go now. I think I know what Brother means about ostriches. I have to call Holly. And Fang. And Devon.

I'm tired of being reborn to the new and improved Emily. I think I'm going to go back to the old me. That Emily was a whole lot happier.

Hugs and kisses,
~Em

Subject: re: WHERE ARE YOU???
From: Emmers@britsahoy.co.uk
To: Dru@seattlegrrl.com
Date: 27 August 2004 11:08pm

Dru wrote:
> *Why haven't you e-mailed me? You can't just leave*
> *me hanging like that! What did you say to Fang and*
> *Holly and Devon? What did they say to you? Are*
> *you and Fang together or not? And just what the*
> *cheese on crows did your father mean about*
> *ostriches get eaten? If my dad said anything like*
> *that to me, I'd call AA and tell them I have a pickup.*

Snort! Snort, snort. That's funny; I'll have to remember that one.

I'm sorry I've been all radio-silenceish, but I've been busy at work, and packing, and talking to Holly and Devon.

Not Fang. And no, it's not what you're thinking.

Holly was the first person I called, because I felt bad that she'd called me and I didn't answer the phone and told Mom I was busy so I wouldn't have to talk to her. I went over to her house, because, you know, if you have to apologize to someone, it means more if you do it in person.

"I'm sorry I've been such a poop," I said as soon as she opened the front door. "I was being stupid, as usual, and you didn't deserve it. So I hope you forgive me and still want to take Buffy and Spike and Beaky, although the vet I took him to said he'll have to be hand-fed for the rest of his life because they can't do a beak transplant and he won't be able to feed himself."

"Oh, Emily," Holly said, her lips all quivery, and I knew she was going to cry, which meant I'd cry, too, because that's all I've been doing this month, cry, cry, cry. Once we got through crying and hugging each other she said that she'd love to hand-feed Beaky. "And you know I could never be mad at you."

"Brother says I've been acting like an idiot. Do you think I've been an ostrich?"

She blinked a couple of times. "Oh. Like you've been hiding your head?" She bit her lip for a minute, then said really fast, "Yes, I do. I know that you're upset about Fang, and you're angry at something I did, and I'm sorry about that—not sorry that I did something, but sorry that you're angry at me for it, especially since I don't know what it is, but yes, I do think you've been a bit of an ostrich, Emily. You're my best friend. It hurt when you wouldn't talk to me."

I waited for her to say she'd never survive without me, but she didn't. I knew then that she would be fine on her own, which was good. "You know, you've really matured a lot since I first met you," I told her. "You climbed castles when you were afraid of heights, you yelled at a bum in Paris when she tried to steal my fake baby doll, and you got rid of your boyfriend when he treated you like dirt. You, Holly Lester, are a tough chick."

She grinned. "I wouldn't be if you hadn't been one, too."

"We are pretty cool, huh?"

"Glacial," she agreed. "Have you talked with Fang? He came by a couple of nights ago, and he seemed very unhappy."

I sighed. "No, I haven't talked to him. There's really nothing to say. I mean, he offered to dump Audrey, but we both know that's not a solution. Fang would feel awful forever, and I couldn't be madly in love with a guy who would dump a girl to be with another girl, even if the other girl was me."

"It's a love triangle," Holly said, her eyes big. "A tragic love triangle—they're the worst kind."

"Tell me about it." I sighed again.

"What are you going to do? Are you going to be proactive and intelligent again? Are you going to make a plan?"

"No!" I said loudly, jumping up and marching over to her bedroom window. "The new Emily is history. The old Emily is back."

"Really?" Holly asked, her eyes getting bigger. "What does that mean, exactly?"

"It means I will do what I would have done before I was proactive and all that stuff. BA."

"BA?"

157

"Before Audrey."

"Oh." Holly thought for a minute. "What would you have done BA?"

"Whined a lot, asked everyone for advice, and then eliminated the problem."

I thought her eyes were going to pop right out of her head. "You're going to have Audrey killed?"

"Oh, yes, I am so Buffy the Audrey Slayer. *Not!* Eliminate as in get rid of her."

"But . . ." Holly bit her lip again. "You said you weren't going to do that. You said it would be unfair to Audrey."

"That was the old Emily. Or rather, the old New Emily. Now I'm the new old Emily, and I say, Hands off; he's mine. Fang makes me happy, and I make him happy, so we're going to be happy, dammit."

"What are you going to do?" she asked, her eyes shining brightly.

"You know, the old Holly would have told me to play nice and not do anything mean. But I get the feeling that the new Holly is going to want to help me get rid of Audrey the Fang-leech."

She grinned. "What do you want me to do?"

"Be my second."

Her grin turned to a look of surprise. "Your what?"

"My second. I read about it in a Regency romance. It seems when guys wanted to fight over a woman, they had a duel. One guy challenged the other, and they shot at each other until one of them yelled uncle, or died. Each guy has what's called a second, which is like a buddy who helps them and stuff. You can be my second."

She gawked at me for a couple of seconds. "You're going to duel with Audrey?"

"Yup. Tomorrow. At Helm's Deep. With swords. It's just her and me, *girlio et girlio,* fighting to see who gets Fang."

"*La vache!*" Holly said. I still think the French are weird for saying, "The cow!" like that, but hey, I've got other things to worry about than what the French say.

"Come on," I said, grabbing my purse and opening the door. "I have to call Audrey and let her know we're dueling so she's not surprised when I beat the pants off her tomorrow."

"This is so exciting!" Holly grabbed her stuff and ran after me. "I've never been a second before! Will I get to fight, too?"

"Sure, you can watch my back and fight off any of the Uruk-Hais and Orcs that she bribes into attacking me."

I trotted down the sidewalk toward the street, heading to the corner where the bus that goes near my home stops.

"How do you know that she'll bribe some of the kids to attack you from behind?" Holly asked as she ran next to me.

"Because that's what I'll be doing!" I answered

with a grin that lasted three seconds before we turned on the juice and ran like bunnies because the bus was just about to pull away.

Audrey wasn't home when I called her, but I left a message with her aunt, and she called back right after dinner. Holly stayed to dinner—and I kept a firm eye on Brother to make sure he did more than just push food around his plate—and made battle plans with me afterward.

"Now, we have to be careful about where to plan the duel," I said, pulling up a picture of Helm's Deep on my computer. I pointed at the curved deeping wall. "If we do it there on the outermost wall, the parents will see, and they'll get mad."

"You think so?" Holly asked, wrinkling up her nose.

"Yeah, because the kids only have plastic swords to keep anyone from getting hurt, and Audrey and I will have real swords."

Her eyes did the bugging thing again.

"That is, we will if you let us borrow your swords."

"But, Em—they're metal! And sharp. Kind of. You could hurt yourself!"

I straightened up and looked down my nose at her. "Me? The daughter of a noted medieval scholar? Brother had swords in our hands before Bess and I could walk!"

"But you don't have one," she said, looking around the library like swords were going to materialize.

"Of course not, why bring them to England? We

have some at home, though, and Brother taught Mom and Bess and I how to do basic sword stuff."

"But . . ." Holly hesitated. "But what about Audrey? She probably doesn't know how to use a sword."

"Then it will be that much easier for me to beat her," I said with a shrug, and went back to the picture of Helm's Deep. "What about here? Behind the keep—"

"The Hornburg."

"Right. Behind the Hornburg. If we have our duel there, no one but the parents on the very far ends of either side will see us, and they'll probably ignore us, because you know how it is when parents watch their kids do a show—all they can see are the ankle-biters."

"But—"

"Ooh, I bet that's her calling back. Hang on. Hello? Hi, Audrey. Yeah, I called. So here's the deal—you've got Fang, and I want him. I'm prepared to fight you for him. No, *fight*. No teeth involved whatsoever, except maybe in some general grimacing and *grr*ing and stuff. No, I don't think it's immature; I think it's very mature. Regency guys did this all the time. It's called a duel, and we'll have ours tomorrow at the battle of Helm's Deep. Holly is my— Excuse me, I didn't laugh at you when you told us how thrilled you were to see Ann Hathaway's cottage! I'm challenging you to a duel! It is *not* silly; it's serious. Winner takes Fang. Yeah? Well, you won't have him for long, missy. Holly, my second, will have a sword for you. If you don't show up to duel with me, you forfeit Fang. What do you mean, or what? If you don't duel . . . um . . ."

"It'll prove she's afraid she won't be good enough to beat you," Holly whispered, her head next to mine as she shared the ear part of the phone with me.

"Yeah! It'll prove you're a total freakazoid and scared to death of me. So be there or else. Two o'-clock. Back of the Hornburg. Bring a second, if you can find one. Later, chick."

"I can't believe you challenged her to a duel," Holly said, looking kind of awed as I hung up. "Over Fang!"

"He's worth it," I said loftily.

"Oh." She frowned. "Will he like being dueled over?"

"Come on; I have to go see how the frogs are do-ing in my drawer." Holly and I ran up the stairs and headed for my room. "As for Fang, he's the one who told me to fight for him. That's exactly what I'm do-ing, so he can't complain."

"Yes, but did he know you meant to *literally* fight Audrey?" Holly asked as I opened up my door. The room was filled with boxes half packed with my stuff, stacks of books and CDs and piles of clothes heaped on every flat surface.

"Good, no underwear! I'll have to call Mr. Wayne and have him come on Sunday to do another séance." I opened the top drawer and checked on the frogs. They were hopping around croaking and not looking too happy at being shut into a drawer with a ghost and lacy bras. I scooped them up and plopped them back in their aquarium. "You guys can have a break for a while. Ew. Frog slime. Great. Now I have to wash my bras again. Oh, well, it's a little sacrifice to make if it takes care of Dermott."

"Emily!" Holly yelled.

I turned to look at her, surprised that she would yell at me. "What?"

She did an annoyed head bob. "Fang? Duel? You and Audrey?"

I wiped my frog-slimy hands on a T-shirt (it was Bess's, bwahahahaha) and said slowly, "No, he probably never really thought I would physically fight Audrey for him, but it's not like I'm going to really hurt her, Hol. I'm just going to beat her at a sword fight. If she accepts the terms of the duel—and I'm really hoping that freakazoid slur will do the trick—then she'll understand that if I win, she has to give him up. It'll all be very honorable and stuff, with no one losing face or anything."

"Oh," she said, and thought about it for a minute. "I guess that makes sense."

"Of course it does," I said, tossing a bunch of socks at her. "Have I ever done anything that didn't make perfect sense?"

She just looked at me.

I sighed. "OK, you don't have to answer that. But trust me, this will work out. I just know it will. Socks go into the box behind you."

Holly helped me pack for a bit; then we had to go downstairs and make the water balloons (instead of arrows) and blood bags for the Helm's Deep thingy. Did I tell you about the blood bags? I know, it's a bit OMG, but they're really cool. When Holly was setting up the battle stuff with the camp people, the kids all said they wanted to have fake blood so they could die really gory deaths. So we're making up tiny little plastic bags of blood that will pop when you squish them. The kids'll tie them under their clothes, and then smash them when they pretend to die. It's going to look great!

I had my last day at work today, which was actually pretty good (it was a payday, too). After lunch I was in the washing room cleaning up and setting some new skeletons soaking so when the girl whose job this really is comes back next week, she'll have a ton of bird toenails to scrape, and in walked Chris G.

"Emily, can you spare a few minutes? I have something I'd like you to see."

I looked at him suspiciously. I mean, wouldn't you? "Is it dead?"

He grinned, which was almost enough to move him back onto my official hottie list, but not quite enough, given that he got excited about dead things like giraffe legs. I'm telling you, Dru, those zoologists are a weird bunch of people! "I'm not going to say anything. Just come with me."

"Wait a minute," I said as I pulled off my gloves and

tossed them. Chris held the door to the outer room open, which is marjorly verboten, since beetles might sneak out. I sighed, gave the bird counter a quick wipe (and avoided looking at the boiling kettles), and toddled out. "Is whatever it is you want to show me a former anything? Like former vole or former fox or former sparrow? Because if it is, I'm going to buy a vowel, Vanna."

He laughed and pushed me out of the mammal room toward the big room of dead birds in filing cabinets. "I didn't know you were so squeamish. This from a girl who has a haunted bedroom?"

"It's a haunted drawer, not a haunted bedroom. Dermott never bothers me; he just has a thing about underwear being in his drawer. I think he was pretending to be a toad, and he kicked the undies out, to be honest, so it's not as if he was at all mean like this Henpecked Harry you guys have. Hey!" I stopped in the middle of the room and glared at him. "You're not dragging me in to see the museum ghost, are you?"

"No." He laughed, and gave me another push.

I walked slowly toward the back office area. "Does whatever you want to show me have legs?"

"No."

I thought of some of the things I'd seen the mammal people doing. "Did it *used* to have legs before you hacked it all to bits?"

He laughed again. "No!"

"Flippers?"

"No."

The office that Helen and I shared was empty, which meant that everyone was probably sitting around the big tables in the Room of Horrors.

"Toenails of any form?"

"If you go into the room, you can see for yourself."

I stopped just shy of the room and made squinty eyes at Chris G. "If there is any level of *ew!* in that room, I will never forgive you."

He just kept grinning and made shooing motions with his hands.

I took a deep breath and walked into the room.

"There she is," Sam said, looking up from lighting candles on a cake. "Happy end of your job, Emily!"

Someone had decorated the room with streamers and balloons and a big sign that said, BON VOYAGE, signed by everyone I worked with. Brent was sitting on a counter next to the radio, which was playing dance music. Chris L and Kia were shoving one of the two tables back out of the way. Even Helen was there, holding out a present. It was a party—for me!

Yeah. You know what happened next. I cried. I couldn't help it; they were all so nice to me! We didn't work at all for the rest of the day. We just ate cake and drank diet Cokes and danced to the music, and I opened my present (everyone had gone in together to buy me a really pretty amber necklace from the museum gift shop), and of course I cried a little more when I said good-bye to them all.

It was a weird place to work, but not really a bad job. Just a little strange at times. And ooky.

Anyhoo, that's what's been going on with me. I'm pooped and I have to go to bed so I won't be tired for my duel tomorrow. Hey, you never told me—what did Felix think of the Prince William flip-flops? Is he impressed that you are so hip that you know stuff like what PW wears? I've lived here for a year, and even *I* didn't know what PW wears on his toesies!

Hugsies and kissies,
~Em

Subject: The countdown . . .
From: Emmers@britsahoy.co.uk
To: Dru@seattlegrrl.com
Date: 28 August 2004 9:30am

And so it begins.

I did that in my best King Theoden voice, BTW.

Countdown: two and a half hours from now the battle commences. Twenty minutes after that, it's Duel Behind the Hornburg, baby!

I'm psyched. I'm pumped. I'm visualizing success like Dr. Nancy recommends. I'm . . . Oh, poop, I forgot to leave my Éowyn necklace out so I could wear it! Must go find it.

Hs and Ks,
~Em

Subject: *sigh*
From: Emmers@britsahoy.co.uk
To: Dru@seattlegrrl.com
Date: 28 August 2004 9:42am

Found the necklace. Also realized that what I thought was just nerves are cramps.
   Why now???
   Crabby, crabby, crabby.

Hs but no Ks because I'm *crampy,*
~Em

Subject: I'm off!
From: Emmers@britsahoy.co.uk
To: Dru@seattlegrrl.com
Date: 28 August 2004 11:03am

Holly's mom is coming to pick me up in a couple of minutes so we can set up the Helm's Deep stuff. Holly is bringing both her swords—the one she got from Ruaraidh for her birthday and the one she already had—and letting me pick which one I want to use.
   Wish me luck! I'm off to fight for my man.

Hugs and smooches,
~Em

Subject: re: Well? What happened????
From: Emmers@britsahoy.co.uk
To: Dru@seattlegrrl.com
Date:29 August 2004 9:39am

Dru wrote:
> never, ever forgive you if you don't e-mail me the
> second you get home, because I'm going to die if I
> don't know whether or not you beat Audrey, and
> what Fang said, and what you did, and everything!
> You have to tell me everything! I just looked. It's
> four o' clock your time. WHY HAVEN'T YOU
> E-MAILED ME? OMG! What if you're dead? What if
> Audrey killed you or maimed you or something and
> you'll never see this? Ack!
>
> E-MAIL ME!!!

Sorry I'm so late in e-mailing you, Dru. It took longer than I thought to get the sword cut stitched up, and then we had to explain to the police, and somehow a TV guy was there with a video camera, and what with the blood everywhere, it was a bit chaotic and all. But we got home about eight, and then we had to feed Brother because he was cranky from not having eaten all day, and having to talk to the police, and going to the hospital to get me.

Then I was so tired, and the meds made me wonky

so I fell asleep while eating, and Mom and Brother had to haul me upstairs.

Anyhoo, I'm up now!

E-mail me when you're up and I'll let you know what happened.

Heh, heh, heh.

~Em

Subject: re: EMILY!!!!
From: Emmers@britsahoy.co.uk
To: Dru@seattlegrrl.com
Date: 29 August 2004 1:50pm

Dru wrote:
> *YOU ARE NOT GOING TO BE MY MAID OF HONOR*
> *IF YOU DO NOT TELL ME WHAT HAPPENED RIGHT*
> *THIS MINUTE, AND I MEAN*
> **RIGHT**
> **THIS**
> **MINUTE*!*

Oh, *there* you are!

Calm down; I just wanted to be sure you were up and about before I gave you the full report of what happened. Are you ready? Comfy? Have your tea and everything? Close your door so your mom won't hear you screaming when you read this, and sit back, 'cause here it comes.

Holly and I got to the part of the campground that we were using for the Helm's Deep thing because it has a big high rock wall in the back, and bleachers along the sides. It's actually a football (aka soccer, but they call it footie here) field, but we thought it was perfect, so that's where we hauled the slides and stuff. Holly's new BF, Craig, was there in his full Legolas garb, and I have to say, he was really tight. He was also nice, but then Ruaraidh was nice, too, so you never know, do you?

Anyhoo, Devon showed up in his knight outfit (he was being Aragorn) and helped us finish setting up, and then the kids started trickling in, and you know how little kids are—they wanted to do everything.

Holly and Craig and the two other camp counselors (Tina and Wendy) started handing out T-shirts and plastic swords to the kids. Parents were at the far end of the camp having tea with the head of the camp and all the camp teachers.

"All right, pay attention, peeps," I yelled as soon as the kids started running around like deranged idiots bashing everything with their swords. I turned over a plastic box and stood on it so everyone could see me. "Holly has named me director of this shindig, so listen up. We have a couple of rules here at Helm's Deep. Rule number— Ow! Hey! That hurt! Rule number one—do not hit Éowyn on the shin with your stupid plastic sword!"

The little monster who smacked my leg grinned up

171

at me. "You have a real sword! I want to see the real sword!"

"No," I told her, touching the hilt of Holly's sword I had strapped onto my Éowyn belt. "Next rule: no throwing water balloons until the battle begins! Rule number three—do not hit each other with your swords. Hey! What did I just say?"

The two kids who had been beating the crap out of each other with their plastic swords stopped. One of them pulled an innocent look I didn't buy for one minute. "What?"

"No hitting each other with your swords! You hit sword-to-sword only."

"Why?" the little snot asked, sticking his tongue out at me.

I stuck mine out back at him. "Because you'll poke your eye out, that's why. Now knock it off! OK, rule number four—do not, I repeat, *do not* squash the blood bags until you're ready to die. That's very important, because once you have blood all over you, you're technically dead, and you have to stop fighting. OK? Everyone understand the rules?"

"You talk funny," another kid said.

"I'm Éowyn," I told him. "I can do whatever I want, and that includes talk with an American accent."

"I want to have a real sword," the first kid said, tugging at the leather scabbard that held Holly's sword.

"Go away, you little snot," I told her. She hit me on the shin with her sword again, then ran off behind the group of kids waiting to get their T-shirts and swords.

"Right," I said, rubbing my shin through my Éowyn skirt with one hand while holding Holly's battle plan with the other. "Here are your assignments: Uruk-Hai group one, start out behind the right bleachers . . . everyone point to the right bleachers . . . no, your *other* right . . . you got it now. You guys start over behind those bleachers, and once you hear Holly give the signal, you come running around the parents and attack the left side of the deeping wall, that bit right there. Everyone got that?"

Fang and Audrey strolled up, Fang in black jeans and a black T-shirt (he was one of the Uruk leaders), and Audrey in pair of tights and long green T-shirt (she was Haldrin, the leader of the elves. She was going to be King Theoden, but I made Holly switch her and Wendy because Haldrin dies early, which means she and I could have our duel in the back without anyone noticing we were gone). Fang gave me a sad look that I couldn't stand to look at too long. Audrey bared her teeth in what I was sure was meant to be a smile, but it looked more like she was planning on biting something—me, probably—so other than baring my teeth back at her, I felt it best to ignore her.

"Uruk-Hai group number two—your leader is Fang. He's the tall guy there in black. Everyone see him?" The minature Uruks in their dirty gray T-shirts and black plastic swords yelled. "Good. Now you guys

173

start at out behind the left bleachers . . . point to them, please . . . you guys are much more on top of things than the other Uruks! That's right; that's left. I mean, that's the left bleachers. OK, so you start there, then run out past the 'rents, and start attacking the wall here, got that? Elves! Where are the elves?"

Ten kids in green T-shirts jumped up and down.

"Great! Audrey is your leader. You guys start out behind the deeping wall, and when the wall is broken, you run out to face the Uruk-Hais. You all die." I smiled grimly at Audrey. She stopped gathering her elves long enough to shoot me a nasty look. "OK, men! You guys in black, divide yourselves in two, please. No, silly, not literally, I mean half of you go on one side, and half on the other side. Holly! Make them divide!"

It took a few minutes before Holly got approximately two groups of kids wearing black T-shirts who were pretending to be humans (and that's truer than it sounds—I swear some of those kids were demons in disguise, and I have the bruises to prove it).

"Right, men—group one, you're mine. We start out on the right hand side of the deeping wall. Men of group two, you belong with Devon over there. He'll show you what to— Hey! I said *no* water balloons until the battle! You make my Éowyn dress wet before it's time and I swear you'll be the one sitting in the cave, got it? Good. OK, everyone, pay attention! Your group leader will pass around the blood bags. Remember! No squashing until you're ready to die!"

As you can imagine, getting those sixty-some kids organized into battle groups was a nightmare. By the time the parents got themselves settled in the bleachers, we were fighting to keep the kids from throwing the blood bags on each other. Even Holly, who as you know is really nice and doesn't yell at people much, was yelling at them to behave, or else.

Before the battle started I dragged Audrey behind the Hornburg and handed her Holly's extra sword.

"You can't be serious," she said, staring at the sword in my hand.

"Absolutely serious. This is a duel." I shoved the sword into her hands.

"You have no idea what you're doing," she said, pulling the sword part of the way out of the scabbard, carefully touching the edge. The swords weren't *sharp* sharp, but they weren't made of plastic, either. I don't think they could cut off anything, but they would hurt if they hit you. "A sword is a dangerous weapon. You don't play with them."

I stared her dead in the eye. "Do I look to you like I'm joking?"

She gave me a long look. "No, you don't. You really want Fang that much?"

"Yes." She pulled the sword all the way out of the scabbard and made a couple of swooping passes with it through the air. I nibbled on my lower lip. "I . . .

uh . . . don't suppose you are willing to give him up? Without doing the duel, I mean?"

She swoop-swooped the sword a couple more times, then sheathed it and strapped the scabbard onto the leather belt she'd tied around her long tee. "After you've gone to so much trouble arranging the duel? I wouldn't dream of it. But I do think you should know one thing before you insist on proceeding with this duel."

I crossed my arms over my chest and raised my chin in Super Éowyn mode. "What? That you love Fang with all your heart, and you'll never, ever give him up?"

"No," she said with a little smile, patting the hilt of the sword. "I took fencing for three years. Is that the horn for the battle to start? Good luck, then. I'll see you after the deeping wall falls."

She toddled off with a truly evil smile, and I took back everything nice I had ever thought about her. I didn't like her in the least little bit. She was evil, pure and simple. She was the anti-Audrey!

"Holly! *Holly!*" I ran around the group of my kids who were standing on the deeping wall waving and yelling at their parents. Holly was standing in the center, directing the last group of kids to hide behind the bleachers. "Holly!"

"What?" she asked, then waved her arm to the left and yelled down to the bleachers. "No, over there. They'll see if you if you stand there! Go back with Fang! What is it, Em?"

"Audrey."

"What about her? Fang! Keep them back behind the . . . Oh, I'll have to go tell him."

"Holly, wait!" I said, grabbing her arm.

"What is it, Emily? We're set to start!"

"It's Audrey—she's fenced."

Holly blinked at me for a couple of seconds; then enlightment filled her eyes. "She hasn't!"

"Yeah. Three years!"

She sucked in her breath, then squeezed my arm. "Don't worry; you'll win. Fang and you were meant to be together. I have to go and keep those Uruks back. Blow the horn when I give the signal, would you?"

I nodded and took the plastic trumpet she shoved at me, walking slowly back to my place, feeling more than a little sick to my stomach. A duel with Audrey had seemed like such a good idea, but now it seemed kind of . . . oh, I don't know, the word *moronic* comes to mind.

Oh, well, nothing I can do about it now, I said to myself as I watched Fang run out to the center of the field and grab one of his troublemaker Uruks and haul him back behind the bleachers. "Fang is mine. Period. No ifs, ands, or buts about it. Listen, kid, I'm crampy and I'm about to fight a duel to what could well be my death. If you hit that other kid one more time with your sword, you're going to be one sorry little Hobbit, got it?"

I guess she got it, because she stopped beating the other kid and got into line.

"Ladies and gentlemen!" Holly stepped out from behind the bleachers and yelled for everyone's attention. "The children and counselors of Never Never Land Camp are happy to present a reenactment of the battle of Helm's Deep. Are we ready?"

Every single kid in the area screamed yes. Holly waved her arms at me. I blew the charge on my plastic horn, which came out more like a really high-pitched raspberry, but no one paid it much attention. The Uruks swarmed yelling and screaming from behind the bleachers.

"Hold it," I yelled at my crew as they jumped up and down, each kid holding a water balloon, two big boxes of extra ammo behind us. "Hold it . . . now! Volley!"

Devon had his kids throwing their water balloons at the same time. The Uruks on the ground racing toward us shrieked and yelled as the balloons found their marks. The parents at the bottom edges of the bleachers shrieked and yelled, too, as they were hit with splashes from the balloons exploding. A couple of kids died dramatic deaths right away, big huge red bloodstains appearing on their gray tees as they slapped their chests until the blood bags tied beneath them burst. Fang's group of Uruks reached the wall first, and found the boxes of balloons we had stashed for them to throw up to the kids manning the walls.

"Incoming!" I yelled as the balloons starting flying toward us. Most of them hit low, but one nailed me right on the chest. I glared out to see who had thrown it, and saw Fang ducking. "Oh! No one water-balloons me and lives to tell about it," I yelled, grabbing one of the reserve balloons and heaving it toward him. (It missed, but you know how bad I am at throwing.)

All in all, it was a pretty good battle. The kids had a great time throwing balloons, popping their blood bags, and dying dramatic deaths, only to get up a few seconds later and fight some more, die again, etc. Audrey and her green elves went down to fight when the deeping wall broke, and my group ran up to higher ground, waiting for our last charge. Craig's zoom down the slide as Legolas was a big hit—they made him do it three more times. By the end of the battle everyone—all the kids, all of us, and about a third of the parents—were soaked in water. The kids were positively gory with blood splashed everywhere. Even I had fake blood on my Éowyn dress from kids falling on me.

When Holly came into the Hornburg to take over the last stand of men, she pulled me behind the cardboard. "Are you sure you want to do this? I can tell Audrey that you hurt yourself or something."

"Are you kidding? That would be so cowardly!" I pushed my hair, which was sopping wet, out of my face (some of the kids seemed to think *I* was a target—the little snotballs). "No, I'm going to do this. I have to do this. This is it, Holly. It's my last stand. Either I do it now, or I lose Fang forever, and I just don't want to do that."

She sighed. "Everything is so black-and-white to you. What about that river thing when you were so metaphysical? You said the river is made up of all sorts of things, and not just one."

"Yeah, well . . ." I bit my lip. I had said that, and I had meant it, too, but now . . . "Oh, pooh, there's Audrey. It's too late now, Hol. Go do the Gandalf thing with the kids while I let Audrey beat the pants off of me."

She looked like she wanted to say something else, but a crash on the other side of the set had her squeezing my hand and yelling, "Good luck!" before she dashed around to finish off the battle.

I walked slowly toward Audrey as she picked her way around the wooden boards that were holding up the front of the Hornburg. She, like me, was wet, with blood on her chest and tights. "Well, here we are."

"Yep," I said, wiping my hands on my skirt. "I guess we're going to do this, huh?"

She did a little half shrug. "You're the challenger. If you'd prefer to back down . . ."

How do I get myself into these things, Dru? Why does what seems like a good idea at the time turn out to be so *not* good? I know I've been doing a lot of internalizing lately, what with the horrible mess my life has been, but at that moment I realized that I have been really stupid about a lot of things. Holly was right—no, wait, *I* was right when I said that whole bit about the river. Just because I was leaving England didn't mean I would never see Fang again. So my life wasn't the way I wanted it to be—that didn't mean it couldn't change later! All along I had been thinking that I had to get things settled with Fang before I had to go home, and as I stood there pulling Holly's sword out of the scabbard and praying that Audrey wouldn't hurt me too horribly, I realized that even if I left England with Fang and Audrey still together, it wasn't the end.

"I'm not going to back down," I said, just wanting to get it over with. She was going to humiliate me, and I was going to have to take it because I had started the whole thing. "Let's do it."

"You're serious?" she asked, pulling out her sword and doing some lightning-fast moves around my sword.

Oh, man, I was *so* dead.

"Yeah. I'm serious."

She zip-zipped her sword around again so fast it was just a blur. "You want Fang that much?"

I wasn't just dead; I was roadkill.

"Yeah. I do."

She spun around in a circle in a fancy move just like someone in a movie, her sword flashing back and forth the whole time while I stood there like a great big lump. "You're in love with him?"

My hair moved with the breeze from her sword.

She was whipping it around my head as she circled me. I closed my eyes and prayed for the world to end. Or a volcano to explode beneath me. Or even a sudden blizzard would be fine. I nodded. "I love him."

She stopped in front of me and I opened my eyes. The point of her sword was resting on my left boob. Right where my heart was. Her head tipped to the side as she looked at me, a slow smile spreading across her face. "Even though you know I'm going to win this duel, you still want to fight for him?"

I started to take a deep breath, realized it would probably cause me to skewer myself on her sword, and instead said, "Yes. Even though I know it was a stupid thing to challenge you to this duel, I still want to fight for him. Sometimes I get a little emotional about things, but I've decided that life is too short to waste. So even though you're going to win today, and I'll have to give up Fang now, I'm not going to give him up permanently. I love him, and he loves me, and someday we're going to be together."

She pursed her lips. "All right, then."

I blinked in surprise as she sheathed her sword. "Huh?"

"I said all right. He's yours."

"What?"

She started walking away from me. I couldn't believe it. She was just walking away? She was letting me have Fang? She wasn't going to fight for him? "*Hey!* You can't do that!"

"I am, though."

I ran after her. "You're giving up? You're conceding?"

She stopped so fast I ran into the back of her. "I'm not giving up; I'm simply not fighting."

"Why?"

"Why?" She laughed, shaking her head. "Emily, you really are the most determined person I know. First you tried everything possible to find another man to interest me, then you challenge me to a duel, and now that you have what you wanted, you want more."

"I want to know why you didn't beat the crap out of me when we both know you could."

She smiled again. "What will you do if I don't tell you? Challenge me again?"

I rolled my eyes. "Do I look that stupid?"

"Perhaps I had a change of heart."

"What, you mean you realized that you wouldn't be happy with Fang after all, so you're giving him up?"

"Mmm . . ."

"Or you realized that he loves me, and not you, and so you're doing the noble thing by letting him go?"

"Mmm . . ."

"Or did you decide that I'm just too cool and hip, and you'd never stand a chance against me?"

She laughed again. "Perhaps it's simply that Fang told me his feelings for you would never lessen, and I realized that trying to change his mind would take too much time and effort?"

"Oh." I thought about that for a few seconds. "That's not noble at all."

"Isn't it? Perhaps there are different types of nobility."

I shook my sword at her. "Oh, no, you're not getting me back into that whole 'there are many shades that make up the river' thing again. Once was enough, thank you very much. Hey, while we're here, can you show me a couple of cool sword things? The only stuff I know is what my father taught me, and that was pretty lame."

"You mean you know how to use a sword?" she asked, her eyebrows going up when I nodded. "Now I am glad I decided not to fight you. I assumed you had no training."

"Nothing formal," I said, doing the little en garde thingy when she pulled her sword out. "Not like you."

We spent about five minutes doing a little sword work, her showing me the classic fencer's stance, and me showing her some of the moves Brother had made us learn. It turns out that she was used to a fencing foil, one of the skinny swords, not the big thick ones like Holly had, so who knows? I might have beaten her.

We got into the whole mock-duel thing. Audrey made a deathly lunge, sending me staggering back clutching my chest, neither one of us really registering the fact that the noise from the battle had stopped.

"I'm dying! Oh, you got me right in the guts! I weaken. I see spots. I die!" My death stagger took me

184

out past the side of the Hornburg, Audrey dancing after me, waving her sword in an impressive manner.

"I'll teach you to try to steal my boyfriend, you wench, you!" she cried, making a lunge toward me.

"Argh!" I yelled, and was just about to fall to the ground suitably dead when two things struck me. The first was that Fang was yelling my name as he climbed up the cardboard battlements to where I was about to fall, and the other was that I really was seeing spots before my eyes.

Spots as in the flash from a camera.

"Holly just told me what's going on," Fang yelled, grabbing me. "How badly are you hurt? You idiot, Emily! I never meant for you to really fight . . . Aw, hell, there's blood everywhere. Dammit, Audrey! You should have known better. Someone call 999!"

My mouth hung open just a little bit as Fang alternated between yelling at me and Audrey, and shaking me.

"I would have found a way, Emily; you had to know that. If you had just let me . . . Is there a doctor here? Will you stop taking pictures; this is my girlfriend who's dying! Where did she hurt you, Em? I don't see where the blood is coming from."

I goggled at him. Then I giggled. I goggled and giggled. I goiggled. "Fang, it's fake blood."

He was busy yelling at Audrey, who stood watching with a surprised look on her face.

185

"Fang!" I said, putting a finger under his chin and turning his head so he looked at me. "I'm not hurt. It's the fake blood. We were just playing."

"What?"

You know, I've never really seen Fang angry before. Aidan, of course, I saw yell all the time. Devon got mad occasionally (never at me), so I'd seen him pissed, too. But Fang? Until that moment when he held me in his arms, yelling at me and Audrey and anyone who came near, I hadn't really seen him angry. I used to think he was the kind of guy who didn't get angry, but the minute he turned his puppy-dog brown eyes on me, I knew I was wrong.

He could get very, very mad.

"Oops," I said, trying for a smile (I failed).

"What do you mean, you were just playing?" he roared at me, his eyes furious. The little sparkly black bits had eaten up all of his irises, which would have interested me enough to comment about, but at that moment I figured I'd better not mention it.

"We were going to hold the duel, but then Audrey relinquished you, so we didn't fight," I said in my *über*-calm voice, the one I have to use on Brother a lot.

"Relinquished me?" I didn't think it was possible, but Fang seemed to be even angrier. "I am not an object, Emily."

"No, but—"

"I'm not an object!" He let go of me so fast that I

fell, and that's how I cut myself. On my own sword, yet.

I don't remember too much after that other than me screaming because my sword was stuck in my thigh, but the guy with the video camera got some really good footage of Fang holding me and kissing my face while I was screaming. I saw it on the news this morning. I'm going to ask if I can have a copy of the tape, because really, how often do you get on TV with your BF kissing you and stuff?

Fang and Holly went with me to the hospital. Holly got sick when they peeled back my dress and saw the gash the sword had made on my thigh (it isn't that bad—just went through the outer bit of my leg, and only took twelve stitches), but Fang stayed next to me the whole time and held my hand, and murmured really nice things in my ear when I went swoony.

Funny, I seemed to get swoony quite a bit, heh, heh, heh. Anyhoo, the police gave me and Audrey a citation for having a duel with real weapons, and they confiscated Holly's swords, which means we both have to buy her new ones.

Gotta run. Fang is coming by for dinner, and Mr. Wayne is coming after for the second séance, and I have to hobble upstairs to find something not packed to wear.

Hugs and big fat kisses,
~Em

Subject: re: OMG!!! Stitches???
From: Emmers@britsahoy.co.uk
To: Dru@seattlegrrl.com
Date: 29 August 2004 9:18pm

Dru wrote:
> *OMG! OMG! OMG! OMG! OMG! OMG!*

That's what I like about you, Dru: you know the perfect thing to say for *every* situation!

> *the most important thing, of course, is did he*
> *kiss you? On the lips? Like a real BF????*

Well, of course he did! Not in the hospital, although he kissed my ear a lot there, but he kissed me when he came for dinner . . . after he yelled at me a bit more for having the duel without telling him.

"It was a stupid thing to do," he said, pacing in front of me, which wasn't easy because it meant he had to walk around all the boxes of stuff that Mom had stacked in the library to get out of the way. "It was irresponsible!"

"I'm sorry," I said, sitting on the couch with my leg up. (There was a big pressure bandage wrapped around my thigh, but I was still supposed to keep my leg elevated for a couple of days.)

"It was ridiculous!" he snarled as he paced by.

"I'm sorry."

"Not to mention dangerous. Did you even think about that?" He marched past me.

"I'm sorry. No. I'm bad. I'd say you could spank me, but that's just too kinky."

"And demeaning to me," he said, not even listening to me as he paced in the other direction.

"I'm sorry about that, too. I didn't think of it that way."

He stopped in front of me, his hands on his hips. "You are never, ever to do it again."

"OK," I said, having to fight really hard not to smile. He was so mad, I knew it would just make him angrier if I told him how adorable he looked when he was lecturing me. "I swear I won't fight a duel for you again."

He glared at me with his nummy puppy-dog eyes, then sighed and knelt down and took my hands. "What am I going to do with you?"

"Well, *not* coming home with girlfriends is going to be my obvious recommendation. Kissing is a close second."

He gave me a look that was remarkably similar to the one Brother gets whenever he has to bail me out of the hospital or tell the police I'm not really insane and/or dangerous. "Emily."

"What?" I asked, figuring I was in for more lecturing.

He leaned forward and brushed his lips against mine. "I love you."

"Yeah, I know," I said, kissing the corners of his mouth.

He growled, which just made me giggle.

"I love you, too. It's been coming on for a long time—I just didn't know it," I whispered, then kissed him like there was no tomorrow. He kissed me back, which was really nice, and then his tongue . . . Whoops! Gotta run. Mr. Wayne is here for the séance. I probably won't get to e-mail you again because Mom wants to pack the computer up tonight, so I guess I'll call you tomorrow when we get in!

Hugs, hugs, hugs!
~Em

Subject: I'm here!
From: Emily@seattlegrrl.com
To: HollyBerry@gobottle.co.uk
Date: August 31 2004 10:36am

Hey, Hol, I'm home again! Yeah, like that's a big shock, huh? I just wanted to tell you what my e-mail addy was, and to let you know that we're here OK, and that my leg is OK, and yeah, you were right, the guys at the airport treated me like I was a terrorist or something because I was on crutches. One man got green when I showed him my stitches, though, so that was fun.

Anyway, I just wanted to say hi, and to tell you how much I miss you already. It's nice to be home, but it's not the same as it was before we went to England. I really miss everything there, especially you. What did your mom say about your coming out for Christmas? My parents said they'd love to have you, and you could stay for the whole Christmas break if you wanted. You think your mom and stepdad will let you come here by yourself? You're all intelligent and proactive Holly now, so I say you tell them that you *have* to come.

How's Beaky?

Say hi to everyone at school for me (except the snotty girls). I'm sure you're going to have a blast in the sixth form, so stop worrying that you won't do well enough to get into a university. You're the smartest girl I know.

Sorry you couldn't come for the second séance, but you didn't miss much. It wasn't very exciting—Mr. Wayne just hummed and swayed for a bit; then he chanted; then he lit incense in the drawer (which was empty).

Finally he looked at the aquarium with the three frogs, and said, "I'm afraid you have not gathered enough toads to effect the cure needed. I do not feel happiness in this room. I sense that the entity Dermott is still bound to the room, tormented by his unnatural fears."

"Oh. Well, we're leaving tomorrow, so more frogs aren't going to happen. Dermott is just going to have to cope with life . . . er . . . death on his own."

"You're leaving?" Mr. Wayne asked, his smile brightening.

I waved my hand around at the last of the boxes. "Well, yeah. Boxes? Moving?" Honestly, it was like the wheel was spinning, but the gerbil was gone.

"Ah," he said, and smiled even more. "Let me just contact one of my spirit guides and see if perhaps the entity Dermott has moved on to a higher plane."

"Uh," I said, about to point out that he just told me that the room didn't feel happy, but before I could, he stopped humming.

"Blessed be! The spirits have spoken! The entity known as Dermott has been released from his mortal bondage!"

"Yay," I said, looking around the room. I know it's silly, but I felt a bit lonely without him. I mean, I've had my undie ghost from the very first day I arrived in England! It's going to be strange not having haunted underwear anymore.

Can you miss a ghost?

Mr. Wayne beamed at me. "It is a blessing, a true blessing. That'll be twenty-five pounds, please."

Oh, hey, before I forget, here's a big "You go, girl" on you and Craig! I'm so happy you're happy! I'm so happy he's happy! I'm so happy you're both happy! Happy, happy, happy!

And hugs, hugs, hugs.
Miss you like mad!
~Em

Subject: re: What do you think?
From: Emily@seattlegrrl.com
To: Fbaxter@oxfordshire.agricoll.co.uk
Date: August 31 2004 10:45am

> *British Columbia Veterinary College accepts transfers*
> *from English universities. It would mean I'd have to*
> *ask my dad for the tuition for the first year, but after*
> *that I could get a job and pay the last two years.*
> *What do you say?*

What do I say? Are you *insane?* BC is just three hours from Seattle, Fang! *Three hours!* We could see each other *every single weekend!* I say that is wonderful!! Better than wonderful; it's miraculous! OMG, I'm so happy I'm going to cry! Here I thought I'd only see you a couple of times a year, but if you transfer to BC, you'll be just a couple of hours away!

You know, the U of BC has a pretty decent physics program, too.

I have to go tell Mom and Brother. They'll be so excited!

Love you more than anything in the world!

Emily

Subject: Oh, *no*!
From: Emily@seattlegrrl.com
To: HollyBerry@gobottle.co.uk
CC: Dru@seattlegrrl.com
Date: August 31 2004 7:54pm

You're not going to believe this—you are just *not* going to believe this—but when I came into my room tonight, my underwear was scattered all over the place.
Dermott came home with me!

~Em the haunted

The Year My Life Went Down the Loo
by Katie Maxwell

Subject: The Grotty and the Fabu (No, it's not a song.)
From: Mrs.Oded@btelecom.co.uk
To: Dru@seattlegrrl.com

Things That Really Irk My Pickle About Living in England

- The school uniform
- Piddlington-on-the-weld (I will forever be known as Emily from *Piddlesville)*
- Marmite (It's yeast sludge! GACK!)
- The ghost in my underwear drawer (Spectral hands fondling my bras—enough said!)
- No malls! What are these people *thinking???*

Things That Keep Me From Flying Home to Seattle for Good Coffee

- Aidan (*Hunkalicious!*)
- Devon (*Droolworthy?* Understatement of the year!*)*
- Fang (He puts the *num* in *nummy!*)
- Holly (Any girl who hunts movie stars with me—and Oded Fehr *will be* mine—is a friend for life.)
- Über-coolio Polo Club (Where the snogging is FINE!)

Dorchester Publishing Co., Inc.
P.O. Box 6640   5251-2
Wayne, PA 19087-8640 $5.99 US/$7.99 CAN

They Wear WHAT Under Their Kilts?
by Katie Maxwell

Subject: Emily's Glossary for People Who Haven't Been to Scotland
From: Mrs.Legolas@kiltnet.com
To: Dru@seattlegrrl.com

Faffing about: running around doing nothing. In other words, spending a month supposedly doing work experience on a Scottish sheep farm, but really spending days on Kilt Watch at the nearest castle.

Schottie: Scottish Hottie, also known as Ruaraidh.

Mad schnoogles: the British way of saying big smoochy kisses. Will admit it sounds v. smart to say it that way.

Bunch of yobbos: a group of mindless idiots. In Scotland, can also mean sheep.

Stooshie: uproar, as in, "If Holly thinks she can take Ruaraidh from me without causing a stooshie, she's out of her mind!"

Sheep dip: not an appetizer.

What's French For "EW!"?

KATIE MAXWELL

Subject: Emily's Handy Phrases For Spring Break in Paris
From: Em-the-enforcer@englandrocks.com
To: Dru@seattlegrrl.com

J'apprendrais par cœur plutôt le Klingon qu'essaye d'apprendre le français en deux semaines.
I would rather memorize Klingon than try to learn French in two weeks.

Vous voulez que je mange un escargot?
You want me to *EAT* a snail?!?

Vous êtes nummy, mais mon petit ami est le roi des hotties, et il vient à Paris seulement pour me voir!
You are nummy, but my boyfriend is the king of hotties, and he's coming to Paris just to see me!

Dorchester Publishing Co., Inc.
P.O. Box 6640 _____5297-0
Wayne, PA 19087-8640 $5.99 US/$7.99 CAN

Please add $2.50 for shipping and handling for the first book and $.75 for each additional book. NY and PA residents, add appropriate sales tax. No cash, stamps, or CODs. Canadian orders require an extra $2.00 for shipping and handling and must be paid in U.S. dollars. Prices and availability subject to change. **Payment must accompany all orders.**

Name: _____
Address: _____
City: _____ State: _____ Zip: _____
E-mail: _____

CHECK OUT OUR WEBSITE! www.smoochya.com
_____ Please send me a free catalog.

EYELINER OF THE GODS
KATIE MAXWELL

To Whom It May Concern:

If you find this letter, it means that I, January James, have fallen down the burial shaft of the Tomb of Tekhen and Tekhnet where I'm spending a month working as a conservator, and am probably lying at the bottom, dead from a broken leg and thirst. . . .

To whoever finds my sand-scoured, withered corpse:

I'm dead. It's the mummy's curse. Don't blame Seth, he was just trying to help, even if everyone does say he's the reincarnation of an evil Egyptian god. He's not. I know, because no one who kisses like he does can be truly evil.

Help! I'm stuck in Egypt with a pushy girl named Chloe, a cursed bracelet, and a hottie who makes my toes curl. . . .

Got Fangs?
Katie Maxwell

I used to think all I wanted was to have a normal life. You know, where I could be one of the crowd and blend in, so no one would know just how different I am. But now I'm stuck in the middle of Hungary with my mom, working for a traveling fair with psychics, magicians, and other really weird people, and somehow, blending in with this crowd doesn't look so good.

Fortunately, there's Benedikt. Yeah, he may be a vampire, but he has a motorcycle, and best of all, he doesn't think I'm the least bit freaky. So I'm supposed to redeem his soul—if his kisses are anything to go by, my new life may not be quite as bad as I imagined.

- -

Didn't want this book to end?

There's more waiting at **www.smoochya.com**:

Win FREE books and makeup!
Read excerpts from other books!
Chat with the authors!
Horoscopes!
Quizzes!